The Dragonbards

THE DRAGONBARDS TRILOGY
by Shirley Rousseau Murphy

Nightpool
The Ivory Lyre
The Dragonbards

The Dragonbards

Shirley Rousseau Murphy

HARPER & ROW, PUBLISHERS

Typography by Joyce Hopkins

1 2 3 4 5 6 7 8 9 10

First Edition

Library of Congress Cataloging-in-Publication Data

Murphy, Shirley Rousseau.
    The dragonbards.

    Summary: Prince Tebriel and his dragonbard companions prepare to fight a fierce battle against the dark forces that threaten their world.
    [1. Fantasy]   I. Title.
PZ7.M956Dr 1988   [Fic]   87-45295
ISBN 0-06-024366-X
ISBN 0-06-024367-8 (lib. bdg.)

For Antonia Markiet

The
Dragonbards

1

I THINK THERE ARE NO MORE SINGING DRAGONS ON
TIRROR. I HAVE SEARCHED WITH MY RESTLESS
THOUGHTS AS SURELY AS IF I FLEW, MYSELF, ACROSS
TIRROR'S WINDS.

From the diary of Meriden, Queen of Auric,
written ten years before the battle at Dacia.

───────⦿───────

The swamp shone dark green, a steamy tangle of
knotted, ancient trees thrusting up from sucking mud.
It stank of rotting leaves and small decaying animals.
Heavy moss hung down, and between the twisted trees,
small pools of water shone. All was silence, the only
sound the hushing whisper of insects, as if this land
had lain untouched for a thousand years.

But suddenly screams shattered the stillness. The
shadows flew apart and the quiet water heaved as a
white dragon came plunging through, bellowing with
terror.

Her iridescent scales shone with sky colors, and her wings were sculptured for flight. But she could not fly. One wing dragged, bloody and broken. Blood coursed down her gashed neck and shoulder staining a trail on the mud. The shouting behind her grew louder. She could hear the pursuing horses splashing and heaving. She fled between trees so dense that the arrow shafts sticking from her sides caught at them, jarring her with pain. Her broken wing pulled her sideways, and her great head swung as she reared to free herself from sucking mud. The shouts of the riders thundered just behind her. She tried again to fly, beating her wings in despair. Then she spun to face her pursuers, belching flame at the dark warriors.

They did not fall back; they fired—their arrows pierced her face and throat. Floundering, screaming with pain, she tried to bring a vision to frighten them, tried to fill their minds with full-grown dragons swooping at them spitting sheets of fire.

But no vision came. She was too unskilled, and the dark powers were too strong. She fled for a small lake between the trees, dragging her torn wing. Dizzy and seared with pain, she crashed heavily through a tangle of willows and dove deep.

She stayed under until her breath was gone, feeling her blood wasting from her, her mind calling out to her nestmates and to a power greater than theirs.

The horsemen drove their mounts belly deep into the lake. When the white dragon surfaced, gulping air, they had surrounded her.

They made quick work of killing her.

The young dragon floated on the bloody lake, her broken wings spread white across the red water. The cheering soldiers raised their fists in victory, their faces twisted into cold smiles. Three of them put ropes on her body and whipped their horses until they had pulled her to a rise of earth.

They cut off her head and strapped it to the back of a packhorse, to carry as a trophy to their dark leader. Finished with her, they wheeled their mounts and stormed away through the mire.

The soldiers were disciples of Quazelzeg, master of the unliving. Three of them were un-men, soulless creatures alien to Tirror. The other five were human men warped to the sick ways of the dark—all of them hated the singing dragons and the human bards they paired with.

2

PERHAPS I AM THE ONLY DRAGONBARD LEFT, EXCEPT
TEB AND CAMERY. I HAVEN'T TOLD THEM THEY ARE
DRAGONBARD BORN. THEY ARE ONLY SMALL CHIL-
DREN, AND IT WOULD BREAK THEIR HEARTS TO KNOW.

The four dragons fought the wind across the open
sea, rising and dropping as the icy blasts beat at them.
They had passed over no land since morning. It was
now past midnight, the freezing black sky pierced only
by cold stars. Below them, the ocean was invisible
except for the shine of whitecaps. The two white dragons shone sharply in the blackness, their sweeping
wings hiding their riders. The two black dragons were
nearly invisible.

Teb slept sprawled along Seastrider's white back,
absorbing the big dragon's warmth. When she banked
across the wind, he jerked awake suddenly, drawing
his sword. But he saw they weren't in battle, and
sheathed his blade again, smiling sheepishly.

The battle is over, Tebriel, Seastrider said silently. *I guess I was dreaming.* He cuffed her neck affectionately. *We're alive,* he thought, grinning. *This time two days ago, I wasn't so sure.*

Nor was I. She changed balance with a subtle twist of her long body and wide wings, and swung her head to look at him. He could feel her excitement, knowing there were young dragons ahead. Somewhere on that frozen land they would find the dragonlings.

They will more than double our number, Tebriel. We will soon be a respectable army.

He stroked her neck, sliding his hand down her gleaming scales. He hoped the four dragons would sense the dragonlings, once they reached Yoorthed's bleak coast. They could never be sure, with the dark so strong, how much their powers would be crippled.

Near to dawn a thin moon lifted out of the sea ahead, reflecting in the blocks of ice that now churned across the restless sea—ice that meant land was near. Teb could not sleep; he stared ahead searching for the first thin line of mountains and trying to sense a hint of the dragonlings.

He was Tebriel of Auric, a prince exiled from his own land by his father's murderer. He had not seen his home in four years. He was young and lean, his skin brown from flying close to the sun. His dark, serious eyes could laugh, but always with a hint of pain, or of anger deep beneath the joy. His dark hair was hidden under a leather hood; his lean hands were muffled in leather mittens. A white powdering of ice had collected along the edge of his hood and across his shoulders, and on the edges of Seastrider's wings.

As he turned to look back at the other four bards, his eyes lost their angry loneliness and his smile came quickly, with a terrible love for them—with a deep love for his sister, Camery. She was nodding between Nightraider's black wings, trying to keep awake. Her long pale hair was tangled around her shoulders and around Marshy. The little boy rode securely in front of her, held tight and sound asleep.

The other white dragon, Windcaller, drew even with Seastrider. Kiri lay sleeping along Windcaller's neck, her arms through the white leather harness, her mittened hands tucked beneath her cheek, her dark hair spilling out of her hood. The two dragons stared ahead searching for land.

Teb watched Kiri stir. *Are you awake?*

Just barely, she thought, looking across the wind at him, yawning. When she turned to look out across the sea, she rose up suddenly, to look. "There's an island! A rock—there among the icebergs."

The four dragons stared, embarrassed that they hadn't seen it first. It was only a hump of granite nearly hidden by the tilting icebergs. Not much of an island, Teb thought, but maybe big enough for the dragons to rest. They headed for it, skidding across the wind.

The dragons dropped to the rock like four huge birds landing on a tiny nest. They coiled down together and began to lick the ice from their wings. Camery wiped sleep from her eyes and slid down from Nightraider's back, holding the sleeping child against her. She stood pressed close to the black dragon, shivering. "Wouldn't a fire be wonderful? And a roast salmon, maybe."

Colewolf slipped down from the other black dragon. *Might as well wish for a whole feast.* He made a vision of hot meat and bread and gravies and pies that made the bards laugh. The older bard could not speak aloud. His tongue had been cut out by the dark leaders years ago. They thought that would prevent him from making visions, for the bard-visions were made by singing—they thought they had destroyed his magic, but they had not. Now, paired with his dragon, Starpounder, Colewolf was as powerful as any of the bards. Even before he had joined with the black dragon, he had been a formidable rebel spy. Colewolf and Kiri—father and daughter—had fought the dark well on Dacia.

Once the dragons had licked the ice away, they thrust their heads over each other's backs, to sleep. Dawn began to lighten the sky. Marshy woke in Camery's arms, shivering. She pulled her cloak closer around him and leaned back against Teb, where he sat in the curve of Seastrider's flank. Teb put his arm around her comfortably. They had been parted for many years, until the war in Dacia had brought them together. She had been a spy for the rebels, working with Kiri and Colewolf. Now, she snuggled close to him. Her voice was hoarse from the cold wind.

9

"Can you find Mama's diary in your pack, Teb? I want to see it; I can't stop thinking of it; I want to read Mama's words. To know that she's alive—nine years since she left us." She turned, in the circle of his arm, to look at him. "The journal of the Queen of Auric. Perhaps the only journal ever written by a dragonbard. And we never knew she was a bard—all our time together, we never knew."

Teb opened his pack and rummaged among a change of clothes and leather packets of dried meat. He drew out the oilskin package and unwrapped their mother's small leather-bound diary. Before they had begun their journey to Yoorthed, he had retrieved it from where he'd hidden it in the dragons' lair. He had had to break the diary's lock.

The first part contained memories of when the two children were small and comments about the dark invaders, how they were moving across Tirror conquering the small island nations. "The part about her leaving us is near the end," he said. "But she thought about it for a long time; the entries are full of it."

Camery thumbed through the pages, whispering Meriden's words as if, by speaking them, she could touch their mother and bring her back to them.

"The wars are flaring across Tirror. Our island nations are being enslaved one by one. The dark invaders sow their seeds of forgetting, until we have no memory of our past. How easy it is for them. With the shape of the past driven from our minds, we are already half

enslaved, and they can quickly defeat us. I bleed for my dear world.

"We have become a world of lost souls, without ties, without history. Soon we will all be slaves of the un- living. And the dark leaders use their slaves cruelly.

"The dragons have been driven out of Tirror by the dark, murdered by the dark, all the dragonbards they could find, murdered. If there are other bards, they have hidden themselves, as I have. I am not proud of hiding. But alone, without a dragon, what can one bard do? Alone, I cannot keep the past alive."

Camery looked up at Teb, her voice catching. He took the diary from her and began where she had stopped.

"Teb and Camery, you may find this diary one day. You are only small children now. I have not told you that you are dragonbard born. I see the longing in you, that terrible restlessness, and I yearn to tell you. But how can I? It would tear you apart to know your true natures, just as it has torn at me, for there is no dragon to join with."

Colewolf sat with his arm around Kiri, his daughter's cheek pressed against his chest, and little Marshy sprawled across their laps. They listened to Meriden's prophetic words and were filled with sadness for her.

"I must leave this world," Camery read, *"and find my way into other worlds. It is the only way I can help Tirror. I know now that the Castle of Doors does exist—a way into those worlds. I have seen it in bard*

11

knowledge, though that knowledge is so often destroyed by the unliving.

"I believe the last dragon on Tirror has gone through the Doors, and I must follow her.

"Why has knowledge of the Castle of Doors touched me now? Why do I remember now? Am I growing stronger in what I am able to recall? Or has the dark revealed this to me, meaning to lure me away from Tirror? But why—what harm can one bard do to the powers that seek to destroy us?

"I dare not go into Aquervell to find the Castle of Doors. The dark holds that continent too strongly. I think there is another Door; my bard knowledge touches it faintly. So much knowledge seems just beyond my reach. I believe there is a Door beneath the sea, in a sunken city off our eastern coast. I believe it joins the Castle of Doors by a warping in space and time. I will sail into the eastern sea and leave word behind that I have drowned. If I can find the Door and get through, and find the dragon, perhaps together we can discover a way to drive the dark from Tirror. Together, we can try.

"What will become of my children? The dark will seek bard children; it will not allow one bard to live. Yet I must leave them. I am so torn and so miserable."

Camery's green eyes filled with pain. "She didn't know—that the dragon she sought was *here*, asleep for so many years. She didn't know that Dawncloud would wake and go to search for her."

Teb shook his head. "Or that Dawncloud would leave a clutch of young behind—our four dragons—that there *would* be dragons on Tirror again."

"And now there are six more," Camery said. "And Mama doesn't know . . . if . . . if she is still alive, to know."

It was Colewolf who had learned of the six dragonlings, from a rebel soldier come recently to their own land from Yoorthed. The man had found a dragon nest atop a rocky isle and climbed to find the empty shells. Later, when Colewolf had given the four bards this information, in vision, his daughter's dark eyes had been deep with yearning, for Kiri dreamed that perhaps her own dragonmate would be among them. And six-year-old Marshy's face had held the same need.

The dragons began to stir restlessly. The bards mounted up, and they took to the sky again. By midmorning, a thin strip of white shone ahead, dividing sea and sky.

They reached Yoorthed at midday. It stretched away below them, an empty plain of ice, broken in the distance by mountains.

They winged along the ice cliff just above the sea, searching for caves. When they found none, they circled up over the plain and came down beside a gully filled with snow. The dragons dug into it with powerful claws, carving a cave out of the wind. Bards and dragons pushed down into the sheltering hole in a tangle. Nightraider rested his black head across Seastrider's white shoulder. Colewolf could hardly be seen under Starpounder's folded black wing. Kiri knelt to kiss her father, then settled beside Windcaller. Little Marshy snuggled against Teb, under Seastrider's chin. Bards and dragons slept as the sun climbed the frozen sky and dropped toward evening.

They woke suddenly. The sense of a creature in pain woke them, a shock of terror that jerked them all out of sleep.

"Dragon!" Kiri cried, leaping up.

Windcaller roared, thrusting up out of the cave to leap into the evening sky. The other three dragons bellowed and rose behind her, circling, sensing out.

3

RATNISBON HAS FALLEN, ON OUR NORTHERN BORDER, AND HALF A DOZEN ISLANDS NORTH OF VOUCHEN VEK. IN SO MANY LANDS, YOUNG GIRLS ARE CHAINED WITHIN THE PALACES FOR THE USE OF THE UNLIVING, AND MEN AND BOYS ARE TORTURED. NO KING OR ARMY SEEMS ANY LONGER ABLE TO DRIVE THE DARK OUT. MY DEAR HUSBAND IS THE MOST VIGILANT OF KINGS, BUT I FEAR EVEN FOR HIM, AND FOR OUR GREEN, LOVELY LAND.

"Young dragons," Nightraider cried, circling above the bards. "Young dragons—to the north. . . ."

"No," said Seastrider, banking away. "One dragon to the south, near that far line of mountains. Can't you sense her there? She is held immobile, filled with pain, dizzy. . . ."

"To the north!" screamed Nightraider, snapping his wings against the red sky. "Four young dragons to the north."

"To the north," echoed Starpounder. "Dragonlings in the north."

Teb stared up at the wheeling dragons, amazed. They seldom argued. But he, too, sensed dragons both to the north and the south. Though from the south, he thought, came the terrible shock of distress.

"To the south," roared Seastrider, huffing flame. She dropped out of the sky, flaring her wings to land beside him. "South!" she bellowed.

"We'll separate," Teb said. "Seastrider and I, Windcaller and Kiri and Marshy will go south."

"It could be a trick of the dark, to separate us," Camery said.

"It could be. We will take care." They might not be able to touch one another's thoughts so far apart, with the dark so strong.

Camery and Colewolf mounted up, and the black dragons headed north. They traveled in silence, searching the ice cliffs.

The white dragons moved fast to the south, Teb leaning down between Seastrider's wings to watch the frozen land. Marshy rode in front of Kiri, his legs tucked into Windcaller's harness. The dragons skirted just above the crashing waves, watching the white cliff for caves, for claw marks in the ice, or any sign that a dragon had passed this way. They were gripped by the bleakness of the frozen land, by the absence of life. Teb looked across at Kiri.

I could have sent you with your father. But . . . I like having you with me.

16

She looked surprised; then her eyes softened with pleasure.

"Cave ahead!" Marshy shouted. "Cave!" The child leaned so far out into the wind that Kiri grabbed his shoulders. A thin opening yawned in the cliff. The dragons circled, to hover beside it.

"Go in," Teb said. "Can you get in?"

Seastrider studied the black hole, sensed the cave's emptiness, and slid into the dark slit folding her wings close as Teb lay along her neck. Windcaller followed, Kiri and Marshy crouching low. The roof brushed their backs.

Inside, the cave opened out into a large, echoing chamber that was almost warm. The riders slid down. Teb took a candle from his pack and struck flint. Flame chased the dragons' shadows up the frozen walls.

"There!" Kiri said, pointing to where claw marks scored the ice. Each set of claws was as wide as Marshy's head—this was a young dragon, not yet full grown. The two dragons sniffed at the marks. Marshy stood on tiptoe and pressed his fingers into the deep scratches. His small hand trembled. His cheeks burned and his gray eyes glowed with a bright, urgent knowledge. Ahead of them somewhere in this frozen land was a very special dragon—the dragon with whom he must be paired. And ahead of them somewhere, his dragon was sick, perhaps dying. He knew this with a deep, instinctive insight.

Deeper in the cave was a tumbled pile of sheep bones and the backbone of a deer. Marshy found where the young dragon had slept, a circle where the ice had melted and refrozen.

"A female," Marshy said, kneeling beside the slick circle to pick up a white dragon scale. All white dragons were female. Each pearly scale was as big as the little boy's palm. The look on Marshy's face was the same as Camery's when she and Nightraider had found each other. It was the same look that had lit Colewolf's eyes when he met Starpounder, after believing for so long that there were no more dragons on Tirror.

Teb watched Kiri and touched her thoughts. She was glad for Marshy; her mind filled with a prayer to the Graven Light that they would find Marshy's young dragon in time. But she was torn, too, with a desolate yearning for that moment when she would join with her own dragonmate. Unsteady questions seared her, and the thought that she might never know her own dragon.

Kiri traveled with Windcaller, but both she and Windcaller searched for another. There was no deciding who would belong to a certain dragon. Such a thing was without choice, established by powers far greater than even bards and dragons could control.

"Please," Marshy said, "we must hurry. She is sick, maybe dying." The two dragons were poised at the mouth of the cave. The bards mounted and headed south again, watching for any movement across the ice plain that was fast dimming toward night. But it was not until the sky was nearly dark, the plain turned to heavy gray, that the two dragons sensed something.

There, Kiri thought, *a gully—that line* . . .

The dragons strained into the wind toward the thin scar that cut across the ice. As they neared it, it widened to a deep ravine. They circled and dropped, hovering, looking down into the cleft, at the shadowed procession that moved along the bottom.

A procession of small men marched there, leading a train of sleds lashed together and pulled by wolves. Bound to the sled, her head lolling, her tail dragging through the snow, was the limp body of a young white dragon.

She can't be dead! Marshy cried. But the little boy's terror filled them.

4

THE DARK SEEKS TO DESTROY THE MYSTERY OF OUR
PASTS WITHIN US—AND SO DESTROY OUR SENSE OF
WHO WE ARE. THAT IS HOW THEY WILL ENSLAVE US—
BY CREATING A RACE WITHOUT SELF-KNOWLEDGE.
ONLY DRAGON SONG CAN STOP THEM. OH, I DREAM OF
SINGING DRAGONS WITH CLAWS AND TEETH LIKE IVORY
SWORDS, TENDER AND AFFECTIONATE DRAGONS, SO
CLEVER AT THE VISION MAKING.

The dragons circled the ravine, driving a sharp wind
down across the procession. The white dragonling's
body rocked limply on the line of sleds. They could not
tell whether she was alive. Marshy stared down at
her, his face white with longing and terror. The fur-
clad soldiers flashed swords and spears, looking up at
them with no hint of gentleness. These were not human
men, but dwarfs. Teb watched them, his hand on his
own sword. If the dragonling was dead, surely they

had killed her. He clenched his knees into Seastrider's sides. *Dive!*

No, Tebriel. They have not hurt her.

I said dive!

Can't you sense it? They are rescuing her. Seastrider swung her head around close to his face. *The dwarf folk mean her no harm! She is near to death. Sick, with something foreign and horrible. It is not* their *doing.*

Seastrider spread her wings and dropped soft as a white flower beside the procession. Windcaller followed. The small men backed away against the snow cliff, their swords drawn but not lashing out. Dwarfs and bards remained still, watching each other. Seastrider said, *They are afraid, Tebriel. But they are not evil.* Marshy slid down from Windcaller and pushed boldly past the swords toward the small dragon. Teb and Kiri dismounted, to face the band's leader.

He was no taller than six-year-old Marshy, broad and stocky, dressed in heavy ermine furs. His crown was a gold band studded with emeralds, sewn into the ermine hood that covered his ears and the end of his pale beard. His lined face was burned by sun and cold. His eyes were so dark, there seemed to be no pupils. He stood with his feet apart, and they were goat's feet, hooved. The tops of his furred trousers were tied around his ankles with rawhide straps. Teb saw the delight in Kiri's eyes, though her face remained solemn. The dwarf king's sword was a blade of fine blue steel, its gold hilt studded with rubies. The other dwarfs, perhaps forty in all, were richly dressed, all armed with splendid blades.

"We are dwarfs of the nation of Stilvoke," the small king said. He eyed the tall white dragons with respect but not, Teb thought, with fear.

"What do you do with the young dragon?" Teb said. "Where do you take her? What has happened to her?"

"The dragon has been drugged, young bard. We found her awash in the sea, her body beating against the cliffs. We hauled her out. There was half a dead seal floating beside her, stinking of the drug cadacus."

Teb looked at Marshy, filled with pain for him. The child was pressed against the young dragon, his arms trying to circle her neck. So the dark also knew about the new clutch of dragons—if the dwarf could be believed. Did the unliving mean to kill the young dragons, or to capture them? He looked steadily at the dwarf king, his mind edgy with questions.

"I am Tebriel of Auric."

There was a murmur of recognition among the dwarfs.

"My companions are Kiri of Dacia, and Marshy of Dacia." Teb studied the dwarf king.

The dwarf looked back, inscrutable as stone. "The dragonling needs warmth, Prince Tebriel. Death is close on her. We are taking her to our cave. Unless you have a better plan."

Teb moved close to the dragon and ran his hand down her neck and side. Her body felt chill and too soft, without the resiliency of life. Marshy pressed his face against hers. Seastrider reached to nose at her; then both big dragons lay down beside her and folded their wings over her and Marshy like a warm tent.

The dwarf band was silent. Their dark eyes had softened. A young woman soldier reached to touch Seastrider's neck, in a subtle gesture of gratitude.

They are good folk, Tebriel, Seastrider said.

Perhaps you are right.

Of course I am right, she said curtly, and dismissed him by busying herself with the dragonling.

Teb watched her with a lopsided grin. She could be infuriating at times.

When the young dragon seemed warmer, Seastrider bit the traces from the wolves, freeing them of their burden, and she and Windcaller took the leather lines in their mouths.

"Our cave is five miles up the ravine," the dwarf king said. The wolves disappeared quickly down the ravine. They had not been speaking wolves, who, out of friendship, might volunteer to pull the sleds. They had been wild wolves, huge and fierce. No one, Teb thought, could easily make friends with such creatures, except dwarfs. Teb reached down from Seastrider's back, took the dwarf king's hand, and the small king clambered up, smiling for the first time. The big dragons set out at a fast pace up the ravine. The dwarf troops trotted double time beside the sled. Teb sat a head taller than the king, his nose filled with the smell of the little man's furs and of woodsmoke. The king sat very straight. Teb could feel his excitement at riding a dragon. Teb began to sense, with bard power, the past of this small man.

These dwarfs had lived under the ice mountains for many generations, mining and smelting, crafting fine metal, and weaving brilliant wool garments and blankets and tapestries from their herds of mountain sheep. Teb glanced across at Kiri. She saw his look and smiled.

I like them. She had lived a long time among street toughs and the soldiers of the dark, bereft of gentleness except among a chosen few. She had lived a long time warily, always on guard. These simple, honest folk pleased her.

They are like the speaking animals, Windcaller said. *They are direct and hide no malice.* The speaking foxes and great cats, the speaking wolves and owls and the otters, were among the bards' dearest friends. *The dwarfs*, Windcaller said, *are just as true.*

Kiri looked across at Teb. *Do you still doubt them?*

Teb stared at her. *I can be wrong. Aren't you ever wrong?*

Yes. But I never expect you to be.

Their eyes held for a moment; then Kiri lowered hers, her cheeks flushing.

Stilvoke Cave was marked by a large triangular opening in the side of an ice-covered dome that lay at the foot of the mountains. It was all the dwarfs and bards could do to get the linked sleds into the cave and slide the dragonling off onto blankets beside the central fire. King Flam was powerful for his size. Once he removed his outer furs, Teb could see that he was not fat, but strong and muscled. The cave smelled of roasting rabbits and baking bread. Folk streamed in from side caves to see the bards and the young dragon.

The two big dragons dug themselves a nest outside the cave, thrusting their heads in through the entrance now and then to look at the dragonling. She had not stirred. The dwarf women made a gruel, which Teb and Kiri fed her while Marshy propped her mouth open. The little boy pressed his shoulder between her upper fangs and with his crippled leg held down her lower jaw, balancing on his good leg. Teb held the big cookpot as Kiri ladled in trenchers of the gruel. Because the dragon had not waked, they got her to swallow only with the power of bard spells. Teb watched Marshy, gripped with the child's painful love for the young creature.

Marshy was an orphan child, raised by the bards and rebels in Dacia. He had grown up stubbornly insisting there were still dragons on Tirror, though the other bards, Kiri and Camery and Colewolf, had no hope. It was only when Teb and the four dragons appeared in Dacia that the older bards knew that he was right. But now, when Marshy had found his own dragon at last, she was close to death.

Kiri's dark eyes searched Teb's, filled with Marshy's pain. This was all Marshy had lived for—to join with his own dragon. "She can't die," Kiri whispered. "Use the magic of the lyre, Teb. Use it now."

They had won the battle of Dacia with the power of the Ivory Lyre of Bayzun. But afterward, the lyre had seemed weakened.

The lyre, carved from the claws of the ancient dragon Bayzun, held all of Bayzun's strength—and all his weakness. It, like the dying dragon, faded easily and built its strength again only slowly.

They had been wary of using it again, saving it for the most urgent need against the dark forces.

"It is needed now," Kiri said. "Use it now."

Teb touched one silver string. The lyre's clear voice rang through the cave bright as starlight, embracing them with promise. He held its cry to whispered softness, for the presence of the dark was ever near. He did not want to draw the dark *here*. He joined his own power with the lyre, and with Kiri and Marshy and the dragons, to make a lingering song of life. Though it filled the cave only softly, it stirred every living soul within its hearing. . . .

Except the dragonling. She did not stir.

Teb looked at Kiri. The lyre's subtle song was not enough. They might alert the dark, but he must make the magic shout, make the cave thunder with the lyre's power, no matter how close were the dark unliving.

Kiri's brown eyes went wide with wonder and with fear, and with a tender, consuming love that Teb sensed, but could not sort out—love for the young dragon, surely.

5

THE DARK CAPTAINS MOVE INTO THE VILLAGES
AND THREE AT A TIME TO TAKE CONTROL, WAR
MINDS WITH THEIR DARK POWERS AND WITH DR
MOLDING WILLING SLAVES. IN THE CITIES THEIF
NIPULATIONS ARE MORE INTRICATE, AS THEY WIN
ALLEGIANCE OF KINGS.

Teb touched the lyre's strings again. All faces
turned to him, solemn and expectant. He slappe
silver strings so the lyre's music raged, summo
wild winds and thunder across Stilvoke Cave.
brought to the young dragon's sleeping mind the p
of dragons, the fearsome passion of dragons, and
tangled past.

When he let the lyre's music quiet to a rhythn
pounding blood, he brought a vision of a dragon
cradled by mountain winds, where sky-colored
reflected clouds, and where dragon babies shatt

their shells and pushed up toward the welcoming sky—
but suddenly the lyre's voice died, sucked away to
silence beneath Teb's hands.

The cave was silent. Only the echo of the lyre's voice
clung.

Still the dragonling did not stir. But Teb could feel
a change in her, subtle as breath, and knew the lyre's
power had drawn her back from the thin edge of dying.
Her body seemed rounder, and her white scales had
begun to shine with iridescent colors. Marshy stroked
and stroked her, murmuring and calling to her. King
Flam began, again, to feed her.

Suddenly she moved one forefoot.

But then she was still again, though she began to
swallow alone, without the need for magic. Teb stared
down at the small ivory lyre. Had he used up all its
strength? Kiri laid her hand on the warm ivory, her
eyes questioning him. He touched one string.

Silence.

King Flam said, "The flaw is in the ivory, young
bards. Do you not know that? It renews itself only
slowly."

Teb stared at him. "How could you know such a
thing?"

King Flam smiled. "When you first found the lyre,
Prince Tebriel, when you broke the spell that hid it,
all Tirror knew once again of its existence."

"Even so, how could you know something we did
not?"

"Has not much of your knowledge been destroyed by the dark powers, Tebriel?"

"It has."

"The dark was surely disturbed when you broke the spell on the lyre. It cannot be pleased that you now wield the lyre's power. I expect the dark unliving would make every effort to destroy your knowledge of the lyre's one flaw. Would it not?"

"But you . . ."

"The dwarf nation is an ancient family, Prince Tebriel. It was our own dwarf ancestor who carved the lyre from the claws of Bayzun."

"You descend from the line of Eppennen?"

"We do. And our knowledge of the lyre, once that knowledge was returned to us, is quite complete."

, Teb tucked the lyre back inside his tunic, cursing the dark that confused the bards' own rightful knowledge. "Will you tell us how you found the dragonling?" he asked.

"We were fishing," King Flam said. "When we came around a bend in the cliff, she was thrashing and struggling across the ice. Her face was smeared with blood, and the dead seal lay next to her, half eaten. We had seen her often in the sky, with her brothers and sisters. We knew the dark soldiers searched for them."

"Quazelzeg's soldiers," Teb said.

King Flam nodded. "Quazelzeg keeps a disciple to practice his evil in this land, but the man is a dull creature. When Quazelzeg wants something particular, he sends his own troops. It is Quazelzeg's ships that search for the young dragons. Surely it was they who left the poisoned seal—surely they who killed this dragonling's nestmate."

Teb's hand paused in midair.

"Killed . . ." Kiri said. "Oh, no . . ."

King Flam nodded. "There were six dragons in the clutch. Three females, three males." He spoke softly, watching Teb, then returned to the rhythm of ladling. "One female was hunted down some months ago by Quazelzeg's soldiers. They caught her in the swamp south of Stilvoke. They . . . beheaded her."

Kiri gasped.

"A trophy for Quazelzeg, I suppose. My folk found her body by a lake in the marsh when they were dragging for crayfish. The land is warm there, heated by the volcano. It is a place that would appeal to dragons. Her wings were broken; she could not have flown from her pursuers."

Kiri turned away, sick.

"They will pay for it," Teb said. "We must get the other dragonlings to safety. Two bards are searching for them now, up the coast."

"The young dragons like to hunt up the coast around the otter colony of Cekus Bay."

"A nation of otters!" Teb said.

"Yes, the otters are good folk. We visit them often. Their waters around Cekus Volcano are warm, the fishing rich. But those waters are shark filled, too. The otter nation is pleased to have the young dragons hunt the predators."

"I lived with the otters of Nightpool for four years," Teb said. "They took care of me when my leg was shattered and my memory gone. They raised me, taught me. They are like my own kin."

King Flam motioned for another pot of gruel. "How did you end up there? What happened to you? We knew that your father, the King of Auric, was murdered."

Teb nodded. "By a trusted officer, a captain named Sivich. I was seven, my sister, Camery, was nine. Sivich's men held us, made us watch him kill our father.

"After that, I was kept chained as a palace slave for five years. Camery was kept locked in the tower.

"But when Sivich learned that a dragon had been seen on Tirror, he decided to capture it, using me as bait. He knew I was a bard though I myself did not know. He saw the dragon mark on my arm. He thought the dragon would come to me. He built a gigantic cage of felled trees and barge chain and chained me inside it."

The dwarfs had pushed close around Teb, to hear the tale.

"I escaped in the midst of battle between Sivich and the rebel leader, Ebis the Black. The dragon herself burned the chains that held me. A soldier pulled me up onto his horse, but his horse was shot and fell on us. The soldier was killed, my leg was broken, and I got a blow on the head.

"I lay in the marsh unconscious until two roving otters found me. They took me on a raft around the coast, to Nightpool. They set my leg and doctored me when I nearly died from fever. They were very patient, as patient as otters can be. I could remember nothing, not even my name."

"They are good folk," King Flam repeated. "I imagine they taught you many of their ways."

"They taught me to dive deep and long and bring up abalone," Teb said, smiling. "They taught me many secrets of the sea and many ways that I value.

"They taught me to eat raw fish, too," he said, laughing. "Your roasting rabbit smells better." He took the weight of the gruel pot from a dwarf and looked around the cave. "There is a strength in this cave, King Flam. A sense of protection and peace."

King Flam nodded. "There are three sanctuaries on this continent, Prince Tebriel. This one is Mund-Ardref."

Once, before the dark unliving invaded Tirror, the cave sanctuaries had been meeting places that brought humans and dwarfs and the speaking animals together in an easy, loving companionship. On the walls of many of the sanctuaries were pictures of the speaking foxes and otters and wolves, the great cats and the speaking owls, and the unicorns—for unicorns had roamed Tirror then, practicing a gentle, healing magic. The dark had driven them all out. It had destroyed the comradery of the sanctuaries and disrupted the nations of speaking animals, so that they hid themselves. Humans had grown sour and afraid, and some had grown obedient to the dark.

There were no pictures in Mund-Ardref, but the walls were carved into shelves crowded with clay bowls and jugs, and into alcoves that held small beds cozy with bright weavings and thick blankets and pillows. The tables and stools were simply made, from stone. It was a comfortable place.

But it was the ceiling that interested Teb. The cave's ceiling curved upward and caught the firelight in a deep metallic glow shot with streaks like silver.

"The roof is iron," King Flam said. "You puzzle over it, and rightly. It is not iron of our world, Prince Tebriel, but comes from some world none of us has ever seen. It is iron that fell into this mountain, crashing down out of the sky thousands of years ago."

Teb's mind touched the knowledge. All history was a part of the bard knowledge, though some was muddled, now, by the dark's powers. He tried very hard, rejecting visions, seeking others, until he could see the world of Tirror before there was life on it. It was a mass of molten stone, with the fires of other worlds blasting into it. He saw a fireball fall onto the mountains of Yoorthed and lodge there. He could see the cave that washed out beneath the iron over centuries.

"The iron has power," King Flam said. "It keeps the dark from us; they do not enter here. We have—"

Marshy's cry stopped the king short.

The dragonling had begun to paw the air. Her eyelids moved. Her nostrils flared. She scented Marshy. He remained very still. She reached out to him.

The dragonling opened her eyes. They were as green as sunlit sea.

Child and dragon stared at each other, their recognition ancient and powerful.

Teb took Kiri's hand and they moved away with Flam and the dwarfs, leaving the child and dragonling alone. The cave darkened as two big heads thrust in to see the baby awake. Seastrider's breath huffed through the cave in smoky whiffs; Windcaller murmured softly; then they withdrew into the snow, their eyes slitted with pleasure.

A feast had been laid out: roast rabbits, broiled mushrooms and roots, a mild amber wine, warm bread, and a fruit called payan that grew in the warm marsh near the volcano. Kiri fixed a bowl for Marshy, but he hardly noticed it. He looked up at Kiri, his face all alight with wonder. "Her name is Iceflower."

Kiri hugged him. "She's lovely, Marshy." The young dragon nuzzled Kiri's hand. Iceflower's face was finely sculptured. The pearly hues of her scales caught the colors of the fire. Marshy's eyes were filled with dreams that now, for the first time, could come true. Kiri kissed him on the forehead and turned away, putting aside her own disquiet.

The food smelled wonderful. She supposed she would feel better once she'd eaten. But she couldn't get her mind from the dragonlings—was one of those young creatures meant to be her own? She tried to touch the dragonlings in thought as they moved across Yoorthed's winds, tried hard to sense that subtle bonding that would mark one special dragon. Her thoughts came back to her empty.

She tried to sense her father and Camery, too, but there was no hint of the two bards. Fear for them chilled her—though she knew it was the enemy doing this, the power of the dark clouding their silent speech. She shook her head, tried to marshal her thoughts, and went to sit with Teb.

As they ate, Teb and Kiri told the dwarfs all they could about the war. On the smaller continents, where Teb and the dragons had been able to bring the past alive, slaves had awakened and remembered their own worth, and had risen to kill their dark masters. But that was only on the small continents. Teb and the dragons, alone, had not been a large enough force to take on the big continents where kings had been mind twisted or replaced. Now that Teb had found the other bards, and now that there would be more dragons, their band would have formidable power—but against a formidable enemy.

"If . . ." Kiri began, then stopped, her voice drowned by the thundering voices of dragons. Bards and dwarfs, jumped up and pushed through the cave door into the moonlight.

The night was filled with dragons, rearing and careening as they greeted each other. Nightraider and Starpounder towered blacker than the sky, in a sparring greeting with Seastrider and Windcaller. Crowding around the big dragons were four strapping dragonlings, three dark males and a female.

From inside the cave came a faint, coughing roar, and Iceflower stumbled out behind the dwarfs, with Marshy beside her. The four dragonlings gawked at her and at the little boy.

"Your bard . . ."

"You found your bard."

"Small . . . he's so small."

"Young . . ."

The dragonlings began to nose at Marshy and sniff him all over.

"You're alive," said the white sister, nosing at Iceflower. "We're very glad you're alive."

"Not dead like Snowlake," said the blue-black dragon.

"I nearly was," said Iceflower.

"We searched for you," said the red-black. "We had no sense of you. The dark . . ."

"They were still searching when we found them," Camery said.

"Iceflower was drugged," Teb said. "A drugged seal."

Camery reached to stroke the sick dragonling. "Did the dark mean to kill you, young one? Or did it mean to capture you?"

"I suspect to capture and train her," Teb said, filled with sharp memory of the time when the dark tried to warp his own mind to their evil way.

Camery touched Teb's cheek and hugged him.

"Did you see any ships?" he said.

"No. The dragonlings saw ships near the otters' bay at Cekus some weeks ago and felt the terrible power of the dark."

"Maybe we can send Quazelzeg's ships to the bottom for the sharks," Teb said, "before we leave this land."

Kiri had moved away, by herself. Teb watched her, feeling sharply her disappointment that none of the dragonlings was for her. He followed her and took her hand, and she leaned her forehead against his shoulder.

"There will be other dragons, Kiri."

"Where? There are no other dragons."

He lifted her chin. "Once, you thought there were *no* dragons on Tirror."

"But . . ."

"There will be other dragons." He put his arms around her. She eased against him, her spirit filled with sadness, needing him, needing his comforting.

"There will be other dragons. Somewhere, a dragon is calling to you. Don't you sense it?"

"I sense it. And I'm always disappointed." She buried her face against his shoulder.

6

THE UNLIVING TAKE NOURISHMENT FROM OUR SUF-
FERING. IT IS THUS THAT THE DARK GROWS STRONG.
THEY ARE THE DARK OPPOSITE OF HUMAN, AND ALL
EVIL FEEDS THEM, WHILE ALL JOY AND LOVE INCITES
THEIR WRATH. THEY CAN DIE, THESE UN-MEN, AS WE
DIE. BUT THEY CAN NEVER TOUCH THE GRAVEN LIGHT.

———◆———

On the continent of Aquervell, deep in Quazelzeg's
fort-castle, two generals and twelve captains met with
their leader in the skull chamber, a windowless stone
room deep beneath the earth. The chamber was lighted
by candles made of human fat. The walls were damp,
the air heavy. Of the fourteen, six were un-men, true
creatures of the unliving. Eight were humans warped
to the ways of the dark. Only in the eyes of the humans
could be seen the defeat they had taken at Dacia.

Quazelzeg watched the group without expression,
seeing every flick of an eyelid, every movement of hand

and turn of head. He was a tall, heavy figure who seemed not made to bend, with pale, tight skin over his heavy-boned face.

"I expect, Captain Vighert, that the present expedition is going better than the last. Better than *your* expedition."

A nerve at the side of Vighert's left eye twitched.

"I do not want another dragon killed." Quazelzeg studied Vighert. "I want them captured. I would not want this to happen again. I plan to use these dragons. You would know that, Vighert, if you paid attention. These dragons are very important. Do you understand me?"

Vighert nodded, stiff and reluctant.

The child slaves along the wall watched the men with blank faces, hiding whatever emotion might be left in them. As Quazelzeg moved around the room, he shoved a dark-haired child out of his way. She fell and did not rise until his back was turned.

"Soon these dragons will belong to us, Vighert. They will bring *our* visions, *our* truth, to Tirror's masses." Quazelzeg smiled, a mirthless stretching of his pale mouth. "And then, gentlemen, we will hold Tirror as powerfully as we hold these slaves." He took up a stick and hit the dark-haired child across the face, for rising before he gave permission. She knelt and kissed his boots. The fingers of a red-haired boy trembled.

"Then *we* will be their ancestors, gentlemen. We will be the ancestors of all Tirror, and they will understand that our pleasures with them are a privilege—that terror is a rare privilege!"

The dark-haired girl and the redheaded boy did not look up, but something subtle passed across their faces. Quazelzeg did not see; he was watching Vighert. He returned to humiliating the captain. "Let us hope that those now on Yoorthed—and Captain Shevek, who is about to go there—are more skilled at capturing dragons than you were, Captain Vighert."

Vighert's face seemed to fold in on itself. Shevek's pock-scarred face looked colorless. The pulse in his neck pounded.

Quazelzeg fixed his eyes on the four who would accompany Shevek. "The dragons are to be chained. Their wings are to be clipped. I want their mouths chained shut so they can't use fire to cut their bonds. I want them drugged and tamed and obedient. Now, does someone wish to express an opposing opinion on the best way to handle young dragons?"

No one did.

"Once the dragons are captive, gentlemen, we will train them with the two bard children."

Vighert said, "No one knows if these children have the skills."

"Of course they have the skills. They have the blood. Both have the mark of the bard." He beckoned the dark-haired girl to him. A tiny brown, three-clawed print marked the inside of her left thigh. He parted the boy's red hair so his neck shone white, and pointed to the same birthmark. "They have the power. With these two, we will create a new history for Tirror—a history that will become more narcotic than cadacus in its power.

"And if this Tebriel and his tribe come here searching . . ." A chilling smile stretched Quazelzeg's face. "If they are drawn here by our powers, we will welcome them.

"For then, gentlemen, we will have all the bards we could want."

"How," said a voice from the second row, a small man with stringy hair tangled across the shoulders of his yellow tunic, "how do you keep a dragon captive?"

"In the caves, of course, Captain Flackel. In the marble caves. No dragon can melt marble."

Flackel stared. "Sivich tried to put a dragon in a cage."

"They tried to *trap* it in a cage, Flackel. You can't trap a grown dragon; you have to capture it in other ways. For instance, with the help of my new pets. *Then* you put it in the cage. A cage it cannot melt."

"It was this Tebriel," said Captain Flackel, "that they used for bait in that trap. He escaped from it."

Quazelzeg gave Flackel a deeply irritated look. "When *I* capture Tebriel, Captain Flackel, he will not escape. Unless, of course, I wish him to do so."

7

THE SEERS AMONG THE SPEAKING ANIMALS WERE RARE
AND WONDERFUL. I FEAR THERE ARE NO MORE ANI-
MAL SEERS LEFT ON TIRROR; I FEAR THE DARK HAS
MURDERED THEM. I WEEP THAT MY OWN CHILDREN
WILL NEVER KNOW THE FRIENDSHIP OF SUCH A ONE.

———◦∞◦———

It was the night after the dragonlings were found
that two of them discovered the dark ship lying hidden
in the marsh to the south, and Teb sensed the captive
animal chained there.

The bards had lingered at Stilvoke Cave, waiting
for Iceflower to grow stronger. The dragons fished for
salmon for the dwarfs to roast; bards, dragons, and
dwarfs spent the evening around a campfire built under
the cold stars, swapping tales. The dragonlings told
how their mother had died, and how, in a last act of
closeness with her, they had named themselves in the
time-old ritual.

Rockdrumlin had chosen his name for a hill formed by ice glaciers. Red-black Firemont took his name from Yoorthed's smoking volcanoes.

The three females found their names in the icy mountains, Iceflower and Snowblitz—and Snowlake, who had been killed in the marsh.

Bluepiper chose his name from the blue snowbird that pecked for worms among the ice floes, its song like the breaking of crystal.

Late in the evening, Teb sensed something amiss, but no one else did. He could not put a direction or shape to it, and as he puzzled over it, it was gone.

Not until well past midnight did the dwarf folk slip off to their sleeping alcoves. The bards and Iceflower stretched out beside the fire. Outside, in the cold night, the other dragons bedded down close together and slept. But Firemont and Bluepiper woke very soon, sensing what Teb had sensed.

They went to investigate. They circled over the ice mountains, puzzled by the pressing sense of terror, and of cruelty, then headed south. They circled the volcano, their nostrils filled with the smell of sulfur that clung around the smoking mountain. The warm swamp lay beyond, sulking in its own heavy steam. They approached it, shivering with the evil they felt there.

They came storming back to Stilvoke Cave just at dawn, wild with shouting.

"There's a ship in the swamp," bellowed Firemont.

"It stinks of dark warriors," cried Bluepiper.

"If you yell any louder," Teb growled, coming awake, "they'll have set sail before we reach them."

The dragonlings lowered their voices, eyeing Teb with respect.

The bards dressed quickly. Teb convinced Marshy to stay in the cave with Iceflower. The rest were soon winging south in the icy dawn, the four bards yawning, trying to come awake, checking again for swords, pulling their hoods around their ears. Kiri looked, sleepily, across the frozen air at Teb. Already a rime of ice crystals covered her hood and the escaping wisps of her hair. Below them, the white mountains caught light from the sun still hidden beyond the sea, the volcano's face stained by the sun's fire. Beyond shone the marsh, its brilliant green shocking against the endless white.

The ship is hidden beneath the trees, said Bluepiper. They circled low. The oaks spread a protective leafy roof over the steaming waters.

Yes, *there*, cried Seastrider. *There* . . .

They could see, beneath the moss-hung trees, part of the ship's bow. They could sense the dark warriors and could sense a terrified captive. Their minds were filled with its silent cry for help.

Someone small, Kiri said, *someone young*. She looked across the wind at Teb.

Teb's face had gone white. His pulse pounded. He could sense the small creature clearly and was filled with its pain and fear. He could see the small body trussed tightly, its broad tail bound to its side, its webbed feet wrapped so tight they were numb. He knew that the otter had no real hope that anyone would hear its silent calls. He gripped his sword as Seastrider dove.

As she flew just above the deck, Teb slid off. Seastrider banked away between the trees. The air was warm and heavy, the deck wet and slick. Starpounder swept down, and Colewolf dropped off beside Teb. It was still night in the tree-covered marsh, the ship too dark for them to see much. They could not sense a guard. The could feel the otter's pain, and they knew something else about it. . . .

Suddenly a shout—hatches were flung open, lamps blazed. They ducked behind a cabin as half-dressed soldiers poured up out of the hold. Weapons gleamed in the light of swinging lanterns. Teb slipped on the wet deck, recovered, blocking swords with his blade. Four came at him. He lost sight of Colewolf, was backed against the rail.

He thrust at a charging soldier, sent him overboard, faced three more. He struck and dodged, sweat running into his eyes. He took a gash on his shoulder. Two more were on him; his weapon was forced back; he felt the barrier of cabin wall behind him.

He kicked one in the groin and ducked, then swung, but the other lunged, its weapon tossed aside, its cold fingers clutching his throat. Its knee slammed into his stomach. He sprawled, his belly torn with pain, and heard crashing overhead.

Branches broke under the diving dragons. Kiri shouted, her sword flashing as she dropped to the deck. She struck down a dark figure. Teb caught a glimpse of Camery; then Seastrider's head filled the foredeck. She snatched up a warrior and crushed it. Dragons towered around the ship, coiling over it so it rocked and heeled. Teb saw fire creeping along the deck from an overturned lamp. He heard a faint, chittering cry.

He ran crouching past the battling swords of Colewolf and two dark soldiers and made for the foredeck as fire leaped behind him.

8

MY HEART BREAKS FOR THE LITTLE ANIMALS WHO
SUFFER AT THE HANDS OF THE UNLIVING. OF ALL
THAT WE CHERISH, PERHAPS TENDERNESS IS MOST
DETESTED BY THE DARK. OH, CAMERY, TEB—YOU MUST
ESCAPE THIS TERROR SOMEHOW.

———·∞·———

The cry came from a locker. Teb jerked the bolt free
and swung the door open. The little otter stared up at
him with terror. It was wrapped in chains so tight it
couldn't move. Its white fur was matted and bloody.
A white otter—a rare white otter.

"I won't hurt you," he said softly, taking it up in his
arms. When he turned, a dark soldier blocked his way.
Seastrider reared, knocked the un-man over the side,
and struck out with fury at two leaping warriors. *Give
the otter to me, Tebriel.*

He shoved the little otter into her open mouth. She
lifted away fast, her wings shattering a mast. Fire cut

along the rail and into the deck as Teb spun around, to fight beside Colewolf.

They killed five more soldiers. When the fire leaped like a wall around them, they fled to Starpounder's back. "Kiri!" Teb shouted as the black dragon lifted. "Camery . . . Kiri . . ."

"Here," Kiri shouted, "I'm here."

"Camery! *Where is Camery?*"

Below them, the ship was a raging fire.

"In the swamp," Kiri cried. "There . . ."

Nightraider flashed by them, breaking trees as he sought to reach Camery. She was high in a tree climbing away from three dark soldiers, her sword flashing as she turned to strike at them. She felled one, but the sword of the second plunged inches from her head. Nightraider snatched him off and crushed him. Camery slashed at the third. He fell. She leaped for Nightraider's back, and he rose straight up, winging through leaping fire. The three dragons sped south over the marsh and beyond it.

Seastrider stood on an icy hill. The young otter lay between her front feet, nearly hidden by her big head as she breathed warm air over him. Teb slid down from Starpounder and knelt beside the small, battered creature. He touched it gently, whispering to it, sickened by the chain that cut and deformed its small body. He examined the lock, trying to force it with his knife.

"They put me in a leather bag," the young otter told him. "I ripped it open, so they chained me." The left side of the otter's face was so swollen, his eye was only a slit. His white fur was the color of dirty rags, matted with dried blood.

Kiri and Camery found mud at the edge of the field and brought it in handfuls, to pack around the chain. When the otter's body was protected, Seastrider cut the metal lock off with a small, quick spurt of flame. As Teb unwrapped the chain, fresh blood started to flow. Camery felt the little otter's legs carefully for broken bones. When she felt his left thigh, he jerked and cried out.

She examined it carefully. "I can't tell whether it's broken. Oh, how could they hurt a little creature so?"

But they all knew how the dark could. The dark partook greedily of such suffering. The little otter had closed its eyes tight against the pain. Its paws were clutched together against its belly. Teb could imagine what plans the dark had for the little white Seer.

"So small," Kiri said.

Camery looked up at Teb. "It was a white otter who took care of you at Nightpool."

"Yes," Teb said, stroking the little otter's ears. "A fine otter, who taught me much."

"What is your name?" Kiri said.

"Hanni. I am Hanni."

"Are you of the nation of Cekus?" Teb asked him.

Tears started in the little otter's eyes. He turned away and wouldn't answer.

When Camery took him in her arms, he snuggled against her and laid his bloody, swollen head beneath her chin against the warmth of her throat.

Colewolf took off his heavy coat, buttoned it up, and tied the neck shut with rawhide cord. He tied the arms together to make a sling around Camery's neck, and they settled Hanni carefully in the warm pouch. Camery's pale hair fell down around him, but when she brushed it back, Hanni grabbed a handful and pressed it against his nose.

"Gold—so gold. Like the chain of my worry stone." He stared at Camery. "They took my worry stone— that was why they wanted me. They tried to make me tell where it came from."

Camery cuddled him close and stroked him.

"What worry stone?" Teb said. "What was it made of?"

"They tried to make me tell. They hurt me. I didn't tell them." He closed his eyes.

Teb said patiently, "What was your worry stone, to make the dark want it?" Most otters' worry stones were only smooth rocks from the sea floor, hung on cords around their necks to keep their paws busy and to crack clams and mussels with.

"It was a special shell. It brought visions."

"I see." Teb studied Hanni's blood-streaked white face and intense brown eyes. He was a very young otter to have survived the dark's torture. "Let's get you back to Stilvoke Cave, where you can have rest and doctoring and a hot meal. You can tell us the rest of the story there."

As they rose on the cold wind, the sun's light glanced up from the ice fields in blinding flashes. Camery held Hanni close to her, snuggling his face under her chin. He was silent, sniffing the wind, staring around him with excitement at the sky full of beating wings.

When they dropped toward Stilvoke Cave, Marshy and Iceflower rose struggling on the wind to meet them. The sick dragonling's wings seemed too heavy for her weak body. "She's mending," Marshy shouted, "she's stronger!" He clung with his arms tight around her neck as she landed stumbling beside the big dragons—but she was trying. For Marshy, she was trying.

In the cave, Kiri and Camery cleaned Hanni's wounds and spread on the dwarfs' special salve, made from moss and oak bark. King Flam brought the little otter a rich soup of dried fish, which Hanni devoured greedily, between yawns.

"You are of the nation of Cekus," King Flam said.

Tears began again, and the little body shook. Hanni tried to speak and could not.

At last he said, "There is no more nation of Cekus."

They watched him in chilled silence.

"The dark raiders came in their ship. Ev-everyone was fishing in the sea." He choked and swallowed, and there was a long pause before he could go on.

"The dark soldiers killed my family. They killed

everyone. With arrows, with spears." Hanni turned his face away. "I wasn't there. I was the only one. . . ."

He collapsed into sobs again, all the pain of his loss and of his long torture shaking him. Camery and Kiri held him between them, murmuring to him.

The young white otter cried uncontrollably for a long time, in a storm of grief. When at last he could continue, he told them how he had been alone at the back of the big meeting cave, engrossed with the small conch shell he wore as a worry stone.

"The conch held a vision," Hanni said. "I was seeing so strong a vision, I didn't hear anything. I heard a little rustling noise once, as if someone was there. I didn't pay any attention.

"When I came out of the cave, the bay was so silent. I didn't hear the voices of my family. There was no laughter, no shouts about what fine fish folk had caught. They—" Tears flowed. Hanni pressed his face into Kiri's shoulder.

"There was blood in the sea. Dead bodies everywhere. The dark ship was just disappearing around the end of Sitha. I stood looking. I knew I must go out there to see if anyone was alive. I went toward the water. They—the dark unliving—had not all gone. One of the dark creatures grabbed me. . . ."

The rest of Hanni's tale was of torture. Small tortures, Hanni called them, because they didn't want him too injured.

"They wanted me to take them where I had gotten

my worry shell. They thought there were more like it. They didn't want me all broken; they wanted me to lead them there and to dive for the conch." He looked up at Teb. "The dark unliving want visions; they want the power of visions.

"They tried to make me bring a vision in my shell. They knew I could. I *wouldn't*," he said stubbornly. "They tried to make me use it to tell where the dragons were." Hanni stared at them. "That was why they came to Cekus, to find the young dragons. When— when no otter would admit they knew dragons, the un-men killed them. Then they thought the shell could tell them.

"When one of them touched my shell, he backed away. None of the others would touch it. One lifted it from me with the tip of his sword while they held me down. They tried to make me tell how much of the vision-making was my power and how much came from the shell. I don't *know* which is which. I wouldn't tell if I did."

"Maybe it's all your power," Teb said.

Hanni shook his head.

"Have you ever brought visions with another shell?"

"Yes. But not as clear as with the conch. It was a rare one, a golden conch. My uncle brought it up from the sea bottom before I was born. He found the chain in the sea. He threaded it through the conch. When I was born white, he knew the conch was for me. When I was big enough, he put it around my neck.

"Now," Hanni said, "now it's at the bottom of the marsh, all burned."

"Are there other ships?" Teb said. "Did they mention other ships traveling with them?"

Hanni shook his head. "They seemed to be all alone." He began to shake again. Kiri cradled the small otter in her arms, and the dwarfs made murmuring noises. King Flam reached to stroke the little creature.

"You can stay here," the dwarf king said. "You can live with us, and you will be our own child."

Hanni cried all the harder.

"That is kind," Teb said. "Or perhaps Hanni will decide to join the otter nation at Nightpool. There is a white Seer there. Thakkur could be his teacher."

Hanni stiffened.

Flam said, "Yes, perhaps he should be among his own people. If he has skills that can be used against—"

"It was Thakkur!" Hanni cried. "His name—the white otter I saw in vision when . . . before they captured me. It was Thakkur. He is in danger—his whole island is in danger."

9

THERE IS AN ISLAND OFF THE COAST OF AURIC WHERE
THE SPEAKING OTTERS LIVE IN SECRECY. I DO NOT
TALK OF IT, OR GO THERE, FOR I FEAR SOME SPY WITHIN
OUR OWN PALACE MIGHT FIND IT. BUT I AM WARMED
TO KNOW OF IT.

Teb held the white otter's shoulders. "What else did
your vision show, of the danger to Nightpool?"

"I saw armies on the mainland. Soldiers were looking toward the otter island and sharpening weapons."

"Has it already happened? Or is it a vision of the
future?"

"I don't know—I can't be sure. I felt mostly their
hatred. I—I couldn't see any more." Tears threatened
again. The little otter was all worn out. Camery and
Kiri fed him more fish soup, then took him away to
tuck him down in one of the sleeping alcoves, covered
with warm blankets. Teb heard them singing to him.

He knew they must go at once. Perhaps only they knew of this, through Hanni's vision. Perhaps only they could save the otter nation.

But how could they travel? Iceflower was not strong enough for the journey of a day and a night across the sea. And they must take Hanni with them, yet Hanni, too, was weak. But Teb felt strongly that Hanni belonged with Thakkur—if Thakkur was still alive.

That thought tore at him, sickening and infuriating him.

Marshy tugged at Teb, staring up, the little boy's gray eyes serious. "Iceflower will be strong enough. You can't leave us. And I won't leave her. She flew today, Tebriel. She is getting well."

We must go together, Colewolf said. *It is the very young, Tebriel, who carry the spirit the dark fears most. We cannot leave them.*

"We'll go together," Teb said. There was nothing else to do. It was too dangerous to leave the dragonling here—the dwarfs could not protect her. They must leave Yoorthed together.

The dwarfs were already packing food and filling the bards' waterskins. The dragons went quickly to make a meal of shark and returned with a rich catch of salmon for the dwarf nation. It was the only gift the bards were able to leave, except for their gratitude and affection.

The bards had a hurried meal. Camery tucked the

sleeping otter into the sling, they thanked Flam and the dwarfs, and mounted up. They lifted quickly, heading east. Snowblitz and the three young males moved out fast, but Iceflower and the older dragons paced themselves against the hard journey ahead. As they swung over the edge of the land, they watched for ships. The dragonlings swept up and down the coast looking, but the sea was empty.

Once they were away from land, the wind blew so cold, their eyes watered and their faces went numb. The young dragons flew close around Iceflower, to shelter her. Her stride was not strong, and near to noon she began to fly unevenly, dropping toward the waves. The dragons settled onto the sea so she could rest. It was not good to be still on this sea; they had hunted huge shark here. Iceflower slept, her wings against the water for balance, her head tucked down on her shoulder. The other dragons swam in a circle around her, the sea crashing up their sides. Teb waited with ill-concealed impatience.

Kiri said, "Maybe she'll be stronger once she's rested." She studied Teb's lean face, red from the icy wind. His urgency to move on unsettled her. "Will you tell me about Nightpool? Will you tell me what it's truly like? Not from bard memory, but—but the way you feel about it."

He looked back at her, half irritated, half touched. It was a painful time to think about Nightpool—yet he couldn't stop thinking about it, seeing the island empty, seeing empty caves and blood staining the black stone cliffs.

"Please, Teb, tell me . . . how it was for you, growing up there." She watched him, saw him ease.

As the dragons rocked close together in the sea, Teb took Kiri's mittened hand and made a song of vision. He showed her Nightpool's hidden valley in the center of the island, with its secret blue lake where the otter babies learned to swim. He showed her the caves carved by the sea into the black stone rim of the island, and inside the caves, the otters' sleeping shelves and the shelves they had carved to hold their sea treasures. He showed her his own cave, his gold coins and rare shells that he had found on the sea bottom, diving with the otters, and the warm gull-feather quilt that Mitta had woven for him. He showed her Mitta, as the little pudgy otter doctored him and changed the clay dressing on his broken leg.

He took her beneath the green-lit sea to swim through shafts of light and shadow beside sunken mountains, playing chasing games with Charkky and Mikk. He showed her Charkky's mischievous underwater tricks and his own fear, sometimes, of the huge moving shadows in the deep. He showed the otters grooming air into their coats to keep warm in the sea, and how they had learned to use the knives and spears Teb helped them steal, and how, reluctantly, they had learned to use fire.

"When I was sick with fever, I slept in Thakkur's

cave. I wasn't any taller than Thakkur then. He used to tell me tales at night before I went to sleep, tales of the sea, of how the whales and porpoises sing, of giant fish deep down, and of ghostly things hidden in the sea. He told of the sunken cities where the old lands were flooded, how you could gather oysters from a palace roof and swim through old, mysterious rooms."

"You were happy there," she said. "Now I know what you were like when you were twelve years old. I wish—I wish I'd been there with you."

"I—so do I," he said quietly. "It was a perfect place, Kiri—learning to swim deep under the sea, all the good shellfish I could eat—that was perfect once I found the flint and a cookpot, so I didn't have to eat it raw."

"It was hard for you to leave Nightpool."

"Maybe I wouldn't have left if I hadn't felt . . . begun to think about the sky."

"Yes," she said, her eyes deep and knowing. "The dreams of dragons—of moving above the world, diving on the wind. . . ."

"Yes." He looked and looked at her. They had known the same longings, had stared up at the sky with the same emptiness.

"But you went from Nightpool, really, to seek the hydrus and kill it. Was it . . . was it terrible?"

Surprised at himself, he shared his terror of the three-headed black hydrus, with its cruel human faces. It had carried him in its mouth, miles out into the sea. He showed her his helpless desperation as he climbed away from it up the exposed wall of the drowned city. He had clung to the top of the wall, surrounded by endless miles of sea, shivering and sick. He let her see how he felt as the hydrus forced its twisted thoughts into his mind, willing him to become its slave.

"But you defeated it. You killed it, Teb." Her look was deep and admiring.

He was silent, remembering.

"When—when you found that your mother had been there in the sunken city—that she wasn't dead after all—how did you feel?"

Teb shook his head. "Angry at first, that she had deceived us, that she let us think she was dead. But crazy with excitement that she was alive. I wanted to go to her, through the Doors to other worlds to search for her, but her dragon drove me back." He showed her the undersea Door, which was linked by a warping of space into the Castle of Doors. He showed the white dragon Dawncloud, rearing over him to make him stay back, then charging through, to search alone, and the Door swinging closed. Neither Meriden nor Dawncloud had returned.

"Endless worlds," he said, "worlds filled with evil."

"There must be good worlds, too."

"Yes. But it is the evil worlds that will watch her as she looks for a way to destroy the dark. How could one bard and one dragon survive among those worlds?"

"She is strong, Teb. Surely the good powers among those worlds will help her." Their look was long and close. She knew his thoughts at that moment as clearly as her own.

Seastrider and Windcaller rocked quietly on the sea, glancing at each other, filled with tenderness for the bards they bore.

When Iceflower woke, they lifted fast, spraying sheets of water, climbing up into a hard, racing wind that battered them but carried them with strength. But still, they had to drop to the sea every few hours so Iceflower could rest. Soon the sun was falling behind them, and they had not made enough miles. They rested as the sky turned red, and when they lifted up through the darkening sky, their flight was even slower. Soon it was deep night, and they were sweeping through low, tattered rain clouds that soaked them with fine mist. Teb could not stop thinking of the danger to Nightpool. And little Hanni was moaning and thrashing, asleep in the leather sling.

Camery said, "He's so restless, and he's been muttering. Shall I wake him?"

Teb looked through the mist toward Camery and Nightraider. "No. What good to bring a vision now? We're moving as fast as we can. Let him sleep." Maybe he didn't want to know. He was already strung tight, tethered by their slowness.

They rested again when the rain slaked. Iceflower was weaker. There was danger that the dark would sense them faltering over the middle of the sea. Teb sent Rockdrumlin and Bluepiper to scout south for a small island where Iceflower could rest more easily. It began to rain hard. Only Hanni, in his leather sling, remained dry. Their minds were filled with thoughts of dark soldiers galloping toward Nightpool. Iceflower tried as hard as she could, stumbling through the sky. When Windcaller moved near to Teb, he could just see the curve of Kiri's cheek between white wings.

You mean to go on alone.

I must.

I want to come with you.

They looked at each other in the darkness. The two dragons swept close, and he reached across space for Kiri's hand, their arms freezing in the cold wind.

Alone, you might not stop the dark's attack. But two dragons, one from each side—dragon fire driving them back . . .

She was right. And he wanted her with him. But he didn't want to endanger her. Yet that was not fair to a bard. A sense of battle filled him, of cold urgency, and when the two dragonlings returned with news of a rocky islet, he looked across at her and nodded.

Seven dragons headed for the island. Seastrider and Windcaller banked away, east, beating fast against the wind, driving themselves on with powerful wings until, ahead in the gray dawn, shone the first small islands, scattered black on the reflecting sea. Kiri pushed back her hood and leaned down, looking. As the sky lightened, the vast mosaic of islands and small continents lay mottled across the gleaming sea, stretching away to their left. Windthorst was straight ahead, Teb's own land of Auric describing the south quarter. They stayed above cloud, looking.

There was no sign of battle, no movement. They swept over Auric's green meadows but saw no figure near the palace, not even a horse. *So empty*, Kiri said. Teb studied the palace, and was filled with homesickness. And though the land might look deserted, they sensed that it was not. The dragons lifted and headed for Nightpool, a black speck off the eastern coast.

They circled the little black island. White breakers licked its seaward cliffs. Nothing stirred on the rocks or in the sea. They dropped low but saw no otter fishing or gathering clams or playing in the shallows. Teb and Seastrider settled onto the water as Windcaller swept away north, along the coast.

Kiri leaned between Windcaller's wings to search, but no army moved below them—they saw no sign of battle, no ships on the sea. The land was as empty as if every living thing had vanished from Windthorst. Not until they banked inland did they see the torn field of battle, strewn with dead soldiers. They dropped low, Windcaller's wings casting shadows across the bodies.

How strange, Kiri said.

More than strange, said Windcaller. There was not one dead horse among the hundred or more dead soldiers—and these were not foot soldiers; they wore the yellow tunics of the dark warriors, who always went mounted.

The palace of Ebis the Black lies to the north, said Windcaller. They circled above the palace, hidden by cloud, and saw horses in the stable yards, people on the streets idling, selling goods; and they could hear music. Surely this city had not been attacked. They headed for Nightpool.

Teb jumped from Seastrider's back to the rocks and climbed the steep cliff. As Seastrider rose to circle, he started along the island's rim toward Thakkur's cave, tense with dread.

The island was so still, the only sound the pounding of the waves. By dawn the otters should be out of their caves, fishing and playing. He paused on the ridge above the entrance to Thakkur's cave, afraid to go down, afraid of what he would find.

At last, sword drawn, he moved down the wet, black cliff, and stood beside the cave door, listening.

The soft, regular huffing of a snoring otter filled the dim space. He grinned and sheathed his sword, then moved inside.

He could see the white blur of Thakkur, sprawled on his sleeping shelf.

"Thakkur."

Another snore.

"Thakkur!"

The snores became uneven huffing. How many times

had Teb heard that sound. The white otter turned over and began snoring evenly again.

"Thakkur! Wake up! The shad are running!"

Thakkur sat up grabbing his sword in one motion, his teeth bared in a fierce otter challenge.

"The shad are running. Come and fish with me!"

Thakkur dropped his sword with a shout of "Tebriel!" and leaped to meet Teb's outstretched arms, nearly smothering him in warm, silky, fishy-smelling fur. "Tebriel! When did you come? What—what has happened to bring you?"

"Must something happen? Can't I just visit?"

"You've been busy winning wars. There's no time for pleasure. What brought you?"

"A vision," Teb said. "A battle—dark raiders. But . . ."

The white otter smiled. "It has already happened. Sivich marched for Nightpool last night. We survived it nicely, thanks to Charkky and Mikk."

Teb sat down on the stone sleeping shelf. "Tell me. I thought you would be—"

"We are not dead, Tebriel. Charkky and Mikk returned around midnight with a band of our best young otters. They tricked Sivich nicely. They alerted Ebis the Black, then stole all of Sivich's horses. They guessed Sivich would attack Nightpool anyway, furious at the loss of the horses. We have badgered him constantly, and he has seen our scouts."

"Well? What happened?"

"Oh, he marched for Nightpool, all right—all those horse soldiers having to go on foot." Thakkur smiled, his white whiskers twitching, his dark eyes deep with sweet revenge. "When Sivich's armies were halfway to Nightpool, Ebis the Black's best horse soldiers surrounded them and killed them."

Teb smiled. "We thought . . ." A commotion in the sea stopped him. Thakkur stepped to the door, sword drawn.

The white otter stood watching uncertainly as, beneath the cliff, the water roiled and heaved. Suddenly a huge white head burst out. Thakkur stared, then said, "Hah!" He stood his ground, looking, and Seastrider stared back at him, her green eyes laughing. A tuna dangled from her fangs. A second later, Windcaller crashed onto the sea from the sky, nearly drenching the island, certainly drenching her rider.

Teb had never seen Thakkur speechless. The white otter's eyes were eager. His whiskers worked with excitement. He seemed to absorb every shining line of the dragons, every reflected color, every curve of their spreading wings. These were the creatures he had seen only in vision, had only dreamed about.

Seastrider thrust her head at the white otter, pushed her nose at his face, and nuzzled his whiskers. Thakkur stroked her nose, his dark eyes bright with wonder.

"You are Thakkur," she said. "You are the Seer of Nightpool."

"I am Thakkur."

"Come on my back, great white otter. I will show you the sky."

Teb had to laugh at Thakkur; the white otter's eagerness made him shiver like a cub. Seastrider swam close to the cliff, holding steady in the waves. Thakkur leaped from the cliff to her back as if he did it every day, then tucked his paws into the white leather harness.

As Seastrider lifted into the silvered sky, bearing the white otter, a shout behind Teb made him turn.

"Hah! Dragons! There are dragons!"

"Thakkur—on a dragon! Oh, my!"

10

ON EKTHUMA, FIVE SPEAKING WOLVES WERE DISCOV-
ERED TALKING WITH SOME CHILDREN. THEY WERE
KILLED AND THEIR BODIES BOUND BY CHAIN TO THE
CHILDREN'S NECKS, AND THE CHILDREN WERE MADE
TO DRAG THEM ABOUT THE CITY. THAT IS THE WAY
OF THE UN-MEN. THEY HUNGER TO DESTROY WARMTH
AND LOVE.

"Dragons in the sea! Hah, dragons!"

Teb stared up the cliff. Two sleek brown faces looked down at him with broad, whiskered grins and dark eyes shining.

"Charkky! Mikk!"

"Tebriel! You have dragons!"

The two otters slid down the cliff to embrace him. They smelled richly of the sea and of fish. Teb knelt and gathered them in, hugging them, laughing with pleasure into their whiskered faces. Charkky pounded his back. "It's a dream!" Charkky shouted. "You really do have dragons! You found dragons!" Mikk winked at him with admiration and looked up at Windcaller banking away over their heads. Kiri sat on a rock, watching them with interest.

"Maybe a dream," Mikk said, "but their wings make real wind. And Teb is real, I can smell him! And who is that sitting on the rock?"

"Kiri," Teb said, putting out a hand to her. She came to stand beside him. Mikk shook her hand.

Charkky smiled shyly when she shook his paw; he turned away and pulled at Teb's arm. "Now that you have dragons, Tebriel, you can drive Sivich from the land. Kill Sivich—"

"I thought Ebis killed him. I thought—"

"Oh, Ebis didn't kill *Sivich*," Charkky said with disgust. "Sivich escaped. *He* was mounted—*he* wouldn't go into battle on foot. He keeps a few horses locked in the stable; we couldn't get at them. We had to leave them behind."

Kiri looked from one otter to the other, first puzzled, then with surprised admiration. "So that was what happened to the horses. You stole them? I saw the battlefield."

The two otters smiled.

Teb said, "If Sivich escaped, we'll find him." He put a stranglehold on Charkky so the young otter thrashed helplessly. With his face close to Charkky's, looking into the otter's dark eyes, Teb said in a low, growling voice, "We will destroy him—together, we will."

"Hah, Tebriel! We'll do that!" Charkky cried.

Teb held Charkky away, laughing. "I want to hear all about last night. How were you sure they were going to attack? How did you get the horses away?"

"We have spies in the palace," Mikk said. "Sivich decided to attack Nightpool when he found out we had been stealing his food and weapons."

Charkky laughed. "He was pretty mad, raving about wiping out Nightpool and killing all of us. Vermin, he called us!"

"So the night of his planned attack," Mikk said, "we loosed the horses and drove them off toward the mountains, to be picked up by rebel troops from the coast."

Teb looked impressed.

"Horses do not like growling otters biting at their heels," Charkky said.

"You're pretty well organized," Teb said.

Mikk's whiskers stiffened with pride.

"What happened when Sivich discovered his horses were gone?" Kiri asked.

"Hah," Charkky said. "He was madder than sin, too mad to scrap the attack. He set out for Nightpool with half his soldiers—a hundred soldiers on foot and only himself and three officers mounted."

Mikk twirled his worry stones. "His foot troops came at double march, and we followed them all the way, running in the darkness. Sivich kept grumbling and muttering about how he would slaughter us all."

"*He* thought he'd just march down the cliff," Charkky said, "and swim his soldiers across to kill us like sheep in a pen."

"Ebis was waiting for Sivich in the valley between Auric Palace and Nightpool," Mikk said. "His mounted men picked off Sivich's foot soldiers like minnows in a tide pool. But," he said more quietly, "Sivich will get fresh horses from the countries friendly to him, and more soldiers. He'll come at us again, you can bet your flippers." In spite of his steadiness, Mikk's dark eyes showed a chill of fear.

"Hah," Charkky said. "Now Tebriel is here! And Kiri! And two white dragons to cut Sivich down from the sky, burn him."

"How long will it take Sivich to get new mounts?" Teb asked.

"A week or more," said Mikk. "By now, the rebel troops will have swum the horses we stole, across the channel to Lair Island for safekeeping. Sivich would never find them there, in that tangle of caves and cliffs. He'll send north for reinforcements."

"We could join with Ebis *now*," Teb said. "Attack Sivich while he has few soldiers and no horses."

"But even without horses," Mikk said, "he's at an advantage when he's fighting from within the palace. He will not come out into the open until he has reinforcements."

Teb nodded. "I don't want to burn Auric Palace. If we wait until new troops arrive, we can wipe them *all* out."

"Yes," Mikk said. "That would be Ebis's choice, too."

"There will be more dragons in a few days," Teb said. "Seven more, and three more bards as well."

"Hah!" Charkky and Mikk shouted together.

"Nine dragons!" Charkky yelled. "The sky will be filled with dragons!"

"And there will be a surprise for Thakkur, too," Teb said. He wouldn't tell them what, though they teased him to find out. He soon left the two otters and Kiri talking about the night's battle. He went along the rim of the island to the caves that looked down on the inner valley, to Mitta's cave.

The little pudgy otter was waiting for him. Teb knelt and put his arms around her.

"You are safe, Tebriel." Her whiskers tickled his neck. "Oh, you are safe." She squeezed him with eager paws, then held him away to look deep into his face, her whiskers twitching with happiness. Teb tried not to see the gray hairs that rimed her muzzle. "Dragonbard," she said softly, her dark eyes and her eager otter face filled with bright wonder.

It was Mitta and Thakkur who had nursed him through his long illness when he hadn't known who he was, had fed him, watched over him, set his broken leg, and changed the dressings on it.

"Dragonbard," she repeated. "And you killed the black hydrus. Oh, I am proud of you, Tebriel." She smiled a whiskery smile. "You will take back your land, now, when you destroy Sivich."

Her assurance, on top of Charkky's and Mikk's, made Teb uneasy. Yet why should it?

He sat with Mitta for a long time, reminiscing, before he took her to meet Kiri and the dragons.

It was the next afternoon that the sky was filled with dragons, as Charkky had said. Mikk and Charkky ran to the highest rock, shouting and pointing. Wings hid the sky. Dragon faces looked down. Dragon teeth and claws shone.

When the dragons dropped onto the sea, they sent waves heaving against Nightpool. As they swam, rocking on the waves, two dragonlings brought Iceflower to the landward side of the island, where the sea was calm. She looked very weak. Mitta saw, and went to her.

Only Thakkur was not watching Iceflower or the circling dragons. He stared past them to where Nightraider rocked on the far swells. Camery was standing up on Nightraider's back, between his spreading black wings. Her arms were raised. She was holding Hanni up, as high as she could. He perched there, looking across the waves at Thakkur. Thakkur looked back, rigid with amazement.

Thakkur dove.

He swam between dragons like a white streak. Before he reached Nightraider, Hanni dove, too. The two otters met in mid sea. They bobbed on the waves, looking. They circled each other, staring. They dove, surfaced, spun in the water, then disappeared beneath the sea. Teb could imagine their flying race deep down in the clear green water.

"No one had to introduce them," Kiri said. "They were kin as soon as they met."

He laughed and took her hand. The two white otters

were together. He felt good, very complete. He put his arm around Kiri, and they watched Mitta, balancing on the rocks, with the waves crashing around her as she touched Iceflower and talked to her.

"What's Mitta doing?" Kiri said. "Iceflower looks so sick."

"She's asking questions," Teb said. Mitta had that stern, doctoring look about her.

When Iceflower rose from the sea, she winged in a dropping glide over the island, and came down in the center valley. Mitta stood on the rock cliff with paws raised, giving orders to a dozen young otters.

Soon Mitta had a fire burning in the valley and a kettle boiling, and she was gathering roots beside the lake. As she steeped her herbs and roots, Iceflower curled up on the meadow with her wings tucked around her. Kiri smiled, watching the efficient little otter. When the brew was ready, Iceflower sucked up the warm potion obediently, and soon her eyes drooped with sleepy comfort.

Soon afterward, a second pot of water was put to boil, and the otters began bringing shellfish. The bards crowded close to the fire, warming themselves, their stomachs rumbling as the good smell of steaming clams and lobster filled the wind. It was not long until they were feasting, at first hungrily, in silence, then with more grace. Marshy ate so much lobster, Kiri thought he would be sick. Hanni sat close to Thakkur, wrapped in Teb's gull-feather blanket. The little white otter, like Thakkur, preferred his shellfish raw. All the otters began asking questions about what had happened in Dacia, though they already knew quite a lot.

News had traveled fast down across the island continents, from owl to fox to great cat to wolf to owl, and at last to Nightpool. The bards listened with excitement to how skilled the animals' network had grown.

Thakkur said, "The news that there are still dragons has given us all new hope. Even the owls are working as one for the first time. Owls are always such loners.

"They have formed cadres and have begun living in communal groups, in the cave sanctuaries. By carrying messages, they have helped the rebel bands come together into a strong army. When news of the dragons and of your victory in Dacia swept the continents, Tebriel, within a matter of days every creature rose to join us."

The otters began to talk all at once, telling how the owls had brought news of boats carrying dark soldiers, and how teams of otters had sunk those boats, swimming deep underwater to pierce the hulls with sword and spear. Or if no otters were near, the great cats or the big speaking wolves had swum out in force, clinging to one side of a boat to flip it, killing the soldiers as they tried to swim ashore. The speaking animals were working so well with the resistance that Teb thought this was nearly like the old times when all speaking folk, man and animal, lived in an active, working harmony.

This very harmony would infuriate Quazelzeg. They all agreed that he would invent new ways to fight them, and a chilling fear touched the little group. The wind seemed to come colder, fingering down inside collars and parting fur, and the surrounding sea seemed all at once an open highway to evil invaders instead of a safe barrier. Little Hanni pushed closer to Thakkur, reaching out a paw. Kiri put her arm around Marshy and drew him near, and squeezed Teb's hand very hard; and she thought, with Teb, that they dare not let fear touch them so powerfully.

In late afternoon the two white otters grew restless. Hanni fidgeted, and Thakkur began a nervous pacing.

The otters and bards had gathered again in the valley, but soon Thakkur was moving back and forth among them; then he and Hanni roved out along the marsh alone, tilting their heads as if they scented something alarming. When they turned to look at the gathered crowd, everyone was watching them.

The two otters left the valley, climbed the black cliff, and stood on its ridge, sharply white against the afternoon sky. The bards and otters rose and followed them, toward the sacred cave.

11

I WILL MISS OUR PICNICS IN THE CAVES OF NISON-
SERTH AND THE JOY IN THE CHILDREN'S FACES WHEN
THEY EXPLORED THERE. THE SACRED CAVES ARE THE
ONLY PLACES LEFT THAT HOLD THE MAGIC OF AN-
CIENT TIMES. THE OTTERS HAVE SUCH A CAVE, AND
IT IS UTTERLY SECRET. ONLY BARD KNOWLEDGE TELLS
ME. I HOPE THEY TAKE GREAT SUSTENANCE IN IT,
GREAT JOY.

The crashing sea echoed across the sacred cave and
flung its spray at the door. The walls of the cave,
shimmering with sea light, were covered with animal
pictures that shifted and changed in the dancing re-
flections—mosaics wrought from tiny shells by ancient
generations.

"It's beautiful," Camery whispered. Kiri and Marshy were silent, looking. Colewolf reached to touch a
shell picture of running unicorns—the unicorns that

had been driven from Tirror by the dark into other worlds. Perhaps they waited somewhere, for a time when they could return, to bring their healing powers to all men and to the other speaking animals.

The otters sat down on the floor, crowding together before the raised dais in a tangle of brown bodies. The bards sat on a stone bench against the wall, close together and hushed. The sacred clamshell stood alone on a stone pedestal at the back of the dais, gleaming in the sea shimmer. A white mosaic dragon reared on the wall behind it, wings spread. The chattering otters became still as Thakkur and Hanni mounted the dais. Hanni, only half Thakkur's height, stretched up as tall as he could, straight and rigid beside Thakkur. The cave was still.

The shell was perfectly curved, like a great and beautifully made bowl. Its inside was the color of a pale sunset, and it was deeply scalloped around its curved top. As Thakkur lifted his paws to it, its blushing surface began to turn smoky. Thakkur's whiskers were straight and still, his thick white tail laid out rigid behind him. Hanni stood exactly the same. As Thakkur muttered softly, shadows began to move across the shell and to gather into an image.

A castle of blood-red stone shone out. Winged jackals paced the top of its high wall, their heads down, their thin lips pulled back to show jagged teeth. Dark soldiers walked in the courtyard. The vision changed to a dim room lit by two greasy torches. Quazelzeg was there, his pale eyes watching the child slaves who knelt before him blank faced. He jerked a dark-haired girl from the line. Her eyes shone with hatred, then were shuttered. When he slapped her, she fell sprawling. When a red-haired boy reached for her, Quazelzeg knocked him to his knees.

Suddenly a light shone deep in the shell, touching the two children as if a hand had reached into the room and thrown sunlight in their faces. The light condensed down into a shape, touching the boy's freckled cheek, the girl's dark eyes with its fleeting image—a three-clawed footprint.

The vision faded.

For a long time, no one moved or spoke. In every mind the mark of the dragonbard blazed, searing away all thought save its wonderful—and terrible—meanings. There were two more bards on Tirror. But they were held as slaves by the dark.

Thakkur and Hanni left the cave without speaking. The bards and otters followed.

Outside, the dragons had come close to the island, rocking on the sea, their eyes blazing as they crowded against the cliff, for their minds, too, were filled with the vision. They stared north toward Aquervell, fierce with the need to avenge the child bards and to rescue them. Nightraider roared, "We will go at once!" and stretched his wings impatiently.

"At once," thundered Starpounder.

"Attack at once," roared Windcaller.

The dragonlings echoed them.

Teb stared at them, scowling. "No! We're not going to storm Aquervell in a great show of flashing wings and tempers. Quazelzeg would kill those two children in a second."

"Nonsense!" Starpounder bellowed. "We will release them before he can touch them."

But they all knew that wasn't possible.

Teb stroked Starpounder's nose. "I think that Quazelzeg does not mean to kill them. He means to use those children. He will torture them, terrify them, in order to train their minds. But he won't kill them—unless we force him to."

"What do you plan?" said Nightraider.

"We must be stealthy, and we must plan carefully," Teb said. "I think Quazelzeg wanted Iceflower because he has the child bards—I think he meant to train the children and the young dragon together."

"Fool—he is a fool," Starpounder shouted. "But I think that you are right, Tebriel."

"Quazelzeg could never train a dragon!" Nightraider roared.

"Never," the dragons agreed, hissing flame.

Seastrider nudged quietly at Teb. "You mean to go alone, Tebriel—just the two of us."

He nodded, reaching to stroke her. "We will slip into Aquervell at night."

"No!" Kiri and Camery said together.

Teb's look silenced them. "Seastrider and I will go. She will stay hidden. I will get into the palace and get the children out—one shadow slipping in and quickly gone."

"And quickly dead," Camery said.

He ignored her. "The rest of you will be here to fight Sivich when he brings the dark forces down on Nightpool. This time, Sivich's attack will be powerful. This time, he will attack Ebis as well. All of you will be needed."

"You won't go alone to Aquervell," Camery said. The set of her face was as stubborn as Teb's. "Nightraider and I are going with you."

"No," Kiri said. "The palace at Auric belongs to you and Teb. It is right that one of you be here to fight for it. Besides, the folk of the resistance know you, trust you. I will go with Teb."

Teb said, "No one is going with me." He saw Thakkur's scowl and ignored it.

Camery said, "You will endanger the children if you go alone. So you will endanger us all. If you were killed, who would get the children out?"

"Camery is right," Thakkur said. "Do not let your terrible hatred of the dark lead you astray, Tebriel. Do not underestimate Quazelzeg and what he is capable of—do not let your pride lead you." The white otter touched Teb's hand. "We are *all* in this. You are not a bard alone anymore. Let the love of your friends strengthen and help you."

81

Teb looked at Thakkur and was torn between rebellion and respect for the white Seer's wisdom.

"Do you remember the prophesy I once gave you, Tebriel?"

"I remember." Thakkur's prediction spoke sharply in his mind: *I see a street in Sharden's city narrow and mean. There is danger there and it reeks of pain. Take care, Tebriel, when you journey into Sharden.*

"You are not invulnerable," Thakkur said. "You must not do this alone."

He felt perfectly capable of doing it alone, of getting the children out secretly and quickly. But he had never turned away from Thakkur's wisdom.

"Do not let pride rule you, Tebriel."

Teb sighed. "I will take one bard. Colewolf—Colewolf's silent speech is strongest. That talent will be needed, with the power of the dark so close."

Thakkur eased his rigid stance and touched his worry stones. Colewolf nodded at Teb's selection.

"No!" Kiri said. "Papa—you are a stronger fighter. You are needed here. You know more about battle tactics than I. I am smaller; I can get into small places."

Teb was silent. He knew very well how clever Kiri was at moving in the shadows of palace passages, at losing herself in attics and niches. But he did not like to take her into danger. He felt a strange and unsettling need to protect her.

"I want to go with you." She touched his face. "All the war against the dark is born of danger. You can't protect someone. I want to be with you."

He took her hand and looked up at Colewolf. Cole-wolf nodded. *There is no way one can skirt danger, Tebriel, either here or in Aquervell.*

Teb clenched his jaw, very torn. "Kiri—Kiri and I will leave at dusk."

Thakkur said, "The otters will prepare dried fish and roots for your packs."

Camery put her arm around him. "Will you draw me a map of Windthorst? I haven't seen it much from the sky, only from horseback—and that so many years ago."

They got a piece of charcoal from the fire and crowded into Thakkur's cave, where the stone floor was smooth and pale. Thakkur and Charkky and Mikk were very interested in the map Teb drew. Marshy curled up on Thakkur's sleeping shelf, absorbing the strategies of war. Hanni had disappeared.

"The mountains curve in deeper here," Teb said, tracing along the center of the continent. "There is a village here, and the river starts here."

"We can station mounted troops along the ridge," Camery said. "In clefts at the foot of the mountains, and along the river." She smiled. "Seven dragons breathing fire should send Sivich's army careening into Ebis's lines like rabbits into a snare."

Colewolf nodded, his gray eyes alight. He was going to enjoy this operation.

"While we're routing Sivich's armies," Camery said, "rebel troops can come up from our coastal villages to clean out Auric Palace and secure it." She looked at

Charkky and Mikk. "Would you two be willing to ride one of the dragonlings, to rally those troops? From the sky you can follow all the action. You have worked with the coastal folk, and you know the lay of the palace."

The two otters gawked, their whiskers stiff with excitement. "Hah," Charkky shouted, "we'll do that! Oh, yes, we will. We'll ride a dragon!"

"I'll get busy on a harness," Kiri said, nearly laughing at the otters' excitement.

Mikk twitched his whiskers at her. "We'll help. We sew very well—Tebriel taught us."

No one noticed Marshy's look of annoyance. No one had included him in any plans.

"Are there still winged jackals in the palace?" Camery asked.

Thakkur smiled. "Not anymore. There were, until the wolves went with Charkky and Mikk to clean them out. They fed their bodies to the sharks."

Marshy left Thakkur's cave before the bards were finished. No one noticed him leave. No one had asked him to help. No one asked what *he* could do to help, or what he wanted to do. He limped along the top of the cliff, scowling out at the sea. He could see the dragons far away, circling over the water, diving for fish.

They hadn't asked because they meant to leave him and Iceflower behind, in Nightpool. He kicked at the black stone path. They thought he was too small and Iceflower still too weak. Well, they were wrong. Iceflower was all well now, with Mitta's potions. And he was a bard, as much as they. He had powers, too. He headed for the meeting cave, filled with anger at the older bards' unfairness, wanting only to be alone.

He didn't see Hanni at first, curled up in a little white ball before the mosaic of the white dragon. When he did see the little otter, he went to sit on the dais, beside Hanni. The otter looked up at him, yawning.

Hanni felt worn out after the vision. He had wanted Thakkur to snuggle him close again and make a bed for him in his own cave, but the old otter had been so busy with the bards, with the terrible business of the captive children. Hanni had come back to the sacred cave and curled up on the dais near the sacred clamshell, watching the play of sea light across the walls.

The two youngsters looked at each other.

"They don't want me to help them," Marshy said. "They think I'm too little." He stared at Hanni. "I *could* help. They will need me."

"How?" said Hanni sleepily.

"I am the only bard small enough to pass for a slave child. They haven't thought of that."

Hanni touched Marshy's cheek with a soft paw.

"I *could* pass as a slave," Marshy said. "I could get them out." He stared at Hanni. "They think I'm too young and too little, and that is the very thing that makes me just right."

Hanni looked hard at Marshy, his dark eyes shining. Marshy looked back, sullen and angry. Hanni rose and approached the sacred shell.

The small white otter reared up before the shell and began to mutter in a soft, chittering voice. Soon the surface of the shell grew dark. Dull lights moved deep within, became streaks, then shafts of sunlight falling between cage bars, to touch the faces of children sleeping on a bare stone floor. Dirty, thin children, chained to the bars by their ankles.

When Hanni began to whisper, darkness tumbled across the clamshell. The next scene was from the sky, looking down upon the red-walled palace. They could see the slave cages in the shadowed corner of the courtyard. Yellow-clad soldiers appeared, driving the slaves out behind lashing whips. Marshy saw the dark, pleading eyes of the girl slave looking up in fear, almost as though she knew they were watching.

Suddenly the little otter turned from the clamshell and hunkered down on his belly, his nose tucked under his foreleg, his eyes squeezed shut, and he was shivering. Marshy stood staring, terrified for him.

Thakkur found Marshy on the dais, kneeling over a limp puff of white fur. The old white otter pushed Marshy aside and scooped Hanni up. He stood looking from Marshy to the clamshell.

"So," Thakkur said.

"He brought a vision," said Marshy.

"It must have been terrible," the old white otter said.

"No worse than before." But Marshy was filled with the hopelessness in the faces of the two slave children.

"Hanni may have seen—or felt—more than you." Thakkur sat down on the edge of the dais cradling Hanni against him, chittering to the young otter. When Hanni didn't stir, Thakkur carried him out into the sunlight and along the path to his own cave and disappeared inside.

Marshy stood irresolutely on the ledge, looking toward Thakkur's cave, then toward the diving dragons. When suddenly the water below the cliff heaved, and Iceflower thrust up through the waves to stare at him, he was very glad to see her.

"You are angry and afraid. Come onto my back."

Marshy scrambled to her back, and she lifted away from the cliff, over the open sea.

High on the wind, she said, "Now tell me what has happened."

"It's the child slaves. I want to go. We can help, but Tebriel will never let us."

She turned her head to look at him. He stared back into her wide green eyes.

"I could pass as one of the slaves. I could get inside to them."

"How would you get them out?"

"With Tebriel and Kiri on the outside, I could. But he won't take me!"

"Have you asked him?"

"He'd only say no. He thinks I'm too small—that you are still too weak. But look how strong you are."

"Tell Tebriel that."

"He won't listen. If they wanted us to help, they would have said so when they were making their plans."

Iceflower bowed her neck. Their minds joined, secure in the same unfolding thought. She gave him another long look; then they flew higher into cloud, to make their plans.

12

I FEEL COMPLETE TRUST IN ONLY A HANDFUL OF OUR
SOLDIERS. GARIT IS ONE. I WOULD TRUST MY LIFE TO
GARIT. IT WAS HE WHO TAUGHT THE CHILDREN TO
RIDE, WHO TRAINED THEIR FIRST PONIES—HE HAS
BEEN LIKE A BROTHER TO US.

The sky was the color of copper, the sun gone behind
the mountains, when Seastrider and Windcaller winged
up between streaks of cloud. Below, on the island,
Marshy and the otters were crowded together, waving. The five dragonlings had settled obediently among
the rocks. *Take care*, they thought. *Take care.*

Soon Nightpool was only a speck below on the burnished sea. Ahead shone the lights of Ratnisbon. Colewolf and Camery were already there, in the Palace of
Ratnisbon, making battle plans with Ebis the Black.
Camery carried the lyre now. Teb would not take it
into Aquervell, so near the dark leaders. If they failed

in this rescue, Quazelzeg must not have the Lyre of Bayzun.

But they would not fail. The unliving would not keep the bard children.

As they winged above Ratnisbon Palace, an image touched them of Camery and Colewolf standing before Ebis's hearthfire beside his tall, broad figure. Outside the palace, the black shapes of Starpounder and Nightraider paced the rocky shore. *Our love is with you,* the dragons thought.

And ours with you, Teb said.

Go with the Light, Camery said.

With the Graven Light, said Colewolf.

Kiri tasted salt on her lips and scrubbed at her dried tears. She hadn't known she was going to cry when she left Papa. They had been parted a hundred times in the war on Dacia—she should be used to parting. Not half an hour ago, Colewolf had held her, stroking her hair. *We are together always, Kiri wren, even when we are apart. You are bone of my bone, child. Blood of my blood—courage of my courage.*

Yes, she thought. Yes, I will be like you, Papa. She looked across at Teb, filled with a sudden and reckless wonder, both that she *could* have the courage of Colewolf, and that she was with Teb, the two of them going to outwit the dark alone. She saw Teb silhouetted against the burnished sky, against endless spaces, and she felt dizzy with excitement. He grinned back at her, and joined his hands in a sign of strength.

The dragons cut north. The continents and small islands lay like black jewels on the copper sea, each circled by a ring of white waves. Their world was so beautiful. The dark must not have all this. Ahead lay three large continents nearly hidden by tall clouds rising like golden mountains. Beyond these was Dacia. They would pass high above her home. She thought of Gram down there, alone, and missed her. There was so much she would like to tell Gram—you could tell Gram anything.

The dragons flew straight into the clouds, where the heavy mist turned the wind chill. Kiri huddled down against Windcaller. They had been flying through the clouds for some time, and it was nearly dark, when Teb twisted around to look back. *We're followed.*

Kiri turned, her hand on her sword, and saw a white shape cutting through the mist. A white owl? No, too big for an owl. As the two dragons lifted, it drew closer, its wings pulling the mist into scarves.

Dragonling, Kiri thought.

Iceflower! said Seastrider.

Lose her! Teb said. The dragons banked away fast. *Go home!* Teb said angrily. *You have no business here.*

The dragonling was silent, beating at the mist with powerful strokes, gaining on them. When Seastrider spun and dove at her to drive her back, they saw Marshy hunched down between her wings.

"Go back!" Teb shouted.

"No!" Marshy cried. "We're coming with you."

"No, you're not. Go back! It's too dangerous. Iceflower is too weak."

"We came to help. She's strong—she's all well."

Teb's anger made him silent. Then, *You can come as far as Dacia Palace. You will stay there, Garit will look after you.*

We don't want to be looked after! We came to help. We don't want to be left somewhere.

Teb said nothing more. Kiri knew he was smiling and saw him shake his head, as much with admiration as in anger. Marshy and Iceflower were a stubborn team. Seastrider and Windcaller moved close to Iceflower, escorting her on between them.

When they crossed the next high mountains, the cold wind pushed up so hard that the dragons were lifted with it. Kiri shivered. Marshy must be freezing. The little boy sat very straight, his chin jutting. When they quit the cloud cover, below them lay Dacia.

The crowded city dropped steeply down the black mountain to the wharfs and the sea. It was lit more brightly than Kiri had ever seen it. As they swept low, she could see that these were not the once-familiar lights of taverns and brothels, but the lights of cottages and shops and street corners where vendors had set up booths. She could see folk strolling the streets, and on one corner they were dancing. Nothing could say more sharply that Dacia had been freed of the dark. The dragons banked across the wind, toward the black mountain.

They passed over the palace courtyard lit with the wavering light of the torches set in its walls. The black mountain ridge rose above the palace towers. The moon was lifting above the mountain, spilling light along the jagged stone. The big dragons headed for the ridge, forcing Iceflower between them.

They came down carefully among boulders. Iceflower dove into a hollow between boulders and huddled there, waiting to be scolded. They could all feel Marshy's defiance. Teb went to Iceflower and laid a hand on Marshy's knee.

"You are not going to Aquervell," Teb said quietly. "You were wrong to follow us. You will—" He was interrupted by a whirring wind and wild screams. The bards spun around, their swords drawn, as the dragons reared, spitting flame.

But then the bards lowered their swords, laughing, and the dragons calmed. A band of tiny owls was sweeping around their heads.

"Elf owls!" Kiri cried, holding out her arms to them.

They landed on her arms and shoulders and head, soft gray owls no bigger than her hand. They flew to Teb and Marshy, and perched along the dragons' backs.

"Who are you?" they hissed. "Ooo-ooo, who has come to the mountain?"

"Dragons," one hissed. "Only one folk bring dragons."

They had spectacled faces, round yellow eyes, and no visible ears. One owl tucked down under Marshy's chin, another beneath Kiri's hair. Their leader hung in the air in front of Teb's face, his wings fanning.

"Ooo-ooo. A name, young bard. What is your name?"

"Tebriel. I am Tebriel."

"And the others?"

"Kiri, of Dacia. Marshy, of Dacia. Who will you take your information to?"

"You tell me, young bard."

"To Garit the Red," Teb said. "You are a fine cadre of guards Garit has chosen."

The owls hissed and fluttered. "Go tell Garit," said the leader. Three owls sped away, over the ridge toward the palace.

It was not long until Garit came galloping up the mountain, led by owls and holding his lantern high. He jumped off his moving mount and grabbed Teb and Kiri up in a wild hug. "Where did you come from, in the middle of the night! Where's Camery? Colewolf? What . . . ?"

"They're fine," Teb said. "They're at Ratnisbon. We'll tell you all of it, all that's happened. But meantime . . ." He glanced toward Iceflower, nearly hidden among the boulders, and the dark lump that was Marshy, sitting on her back.

Garit stared. His silence was long, broken by a sigh of astonished pleasure. He went to stand before the young dragon, looking up at Marshy.

"You have found your dragon," he said softly. "You have found each other."

Marshy nodded but remained quiet.

Garit held out his arms. "What's wrong?"

Marshy looked down unhappily, then slid down into Garit's hug, hiding his face against Garit's heavy red beard.

"They followed us secretly," Teb said. "They are waiting to be scolded. They were supposed to stay in Nightpool." He put a hand on Marshy's shoulder. "We'll talk about it later."

"Come," Garit said. "Come down to the hall and get warm."

The dragons took to the sky to hunt their supper, Iceflower tagging behind. The three bards moved down the dark mountain beside Garit's mare.

"Iceflower will get her scolding privately," Kiri said.

Teb nodded. Garit reached down from his mare and tousled Kiri's hair. The tiny owls banked and dove around them. When they reached the palace stables, the owls perched on rafters and barn doors while Garit unsaddled the mare.

Walking from stables to palace, Kiri stared up at the black stone wall uneasily, filled with memories of her years as a palace page. Too many errands through those dark rooms, too many times when she had stood hidden, spying, terrified of being caught. The palace was a maze of dark passages and heavy draperies where anyone, or anything, could be concealed. How many times she had crouched behind some piece of heavy furniture, listening to the plans of the dark leaders.

She could not shake the sense of King Sardira here; her mind was filled with his frightening captains moving through the shadowed halls.

But Sardira was dead; his officers were dead. Teb took her hand, and she walked more easily beside him, up the stone steps.

Garit flung the doors open, and she had taken two steps into the hall before she caught her breath, staring.

The hall was not the same.

It was not dark and crowded and depressing; it was not at all the same. The walls had been painted white. There was little furniture; no draperies concealed the tall windows, now lit warmly by the courtyard torches. The floor of the huge square hall had been scrubbed to a pale, buff stone, and just a few simple pieces of furniture stood before the fire, with a clay jug of leafy branches decorating the hearth. The far end of the room held a long pine table with benches, clean and bare against the white walls.

Garit stood by the mantel watching her, looking for her approval.

"It's wonderful!" she said. "It's been only a few days since we left, but you've made it beautiful."

Garit smiled hugely, his red beard and hair as bright as the flames. He was so pleased that she liked the hall, and so glad to see them, he couldn't stop smiling. His great bulk and broad shoulders were clad in the same kind of familiar leathers that she had known since childhood.

"We've whitewashed the main sleeping chambers, too," he said, "and closed off the darkest rooms and passages." Many of the palace rooms were black stone caves carved into the mountain. "The whole city has helped. We moved all the orphan children, and the children who were slaves, into the royal chambers. Many of the rebel soldiers have moved in, too." He smiled with accomplishment. "We're turning it into a regular fortress of young soldiers. But come, help me get some seedcakes and tea."

She tucked her arm in his and tried to copy his long strides as she had used to do when she was little. It was easier now. His voice was filled with happiness as he told her about the children.

"They're beginning to get their strength back, though it will take many of them a long time to get over the effects of the drugs the dark had fed them. They're very pale and weak." He shook his head. "Some can hardly keep their food down. They remember nothing but being chained and beaten, being hungry and cold and hurt. They were delighted just to have beds of their own and warm covers."

Kiri put cups on a tray, glancing up at Garit. It was wonderful to feel this kind of caring in the palace where, only days before, Sardira's dull, heavy cruelty had festered.

"Most of the children want to train as soldiers," Garit said as he cut bread and cheese and cold meat. "We're still rounding up the horses that ran off during battle. We're going to get the farms working again. But come, the hot tea will warm you. Put that pie on the tray, with the seedcakes. I want to hear all that has happened. I want to hear how you found the young dragons. How many are there? Oh, I have a hundred questions."

Back in the hall, the little owls crowded around the hearth, chattering, waiting eagerly to pick seeds from the round, flat cakes. Garit and Kiri set down their trays on a low table before the fire. "Come," he said, "make yourselves comfortable." He put his arm around Kiri, laughing down at her. "You're as fidgety as a colt. Some owls have gone to fetch Gram. Go on, Kiri—go meet her."

Kiri hugged him and ran out, her eager mind filled with Gram. It had been only a few days, but it seemed like forever. She ran across the courtyard and through the main gate, and was halfway down the path when a flight of owls burst out of the darkness. Right behind them was Gram, her cloak blowing away from her thin body as she hurried along into the flickering torchlight.

"Gram! Oh, Gram . . ." Kiri grabbed Gram up in a wild hug, swallowing back tears. Gram squeezed her so hard, Kiri forgot how frail the old woman was. Then Gram held her away, to look her over.

"Only a few days," Gram said, "but you look different." She studied Kiri's face. "You look—oh, Kiri—all grown up. You look wonderful." Gram's tears started, but she was smiling. "You look very like what you are. The power—the power of the bard shows, Kiri." Gram's eyes were bright and laughing. "The power of the sky is in you. And the magic."

When Marshy was warm and fed and yawning, Teb sat down close to him and studied his serious face. Garit left them, to brew more tea.

"Well," Teb said, "let's hear it."

"I mean to go with you, to Aquervell."

"You didn't say anything when we were making plans."

"You wouldn't have listened. You wouldn't have let me. You would have said I am too small and Iceflower is too weak."

"There is some truth in that."

The little boy looked evenly at Teb. His fists were clenched. "I must go. I am needed." Teb remained still, caught by Marshy's urgency.

"I am a child, Tebriel. And that is why I must go."

Teb waited.

"If I was chained among the slave children, I would look just like one of them."

Teb's jaw tightened.

"It might be the only way," Marshy said.

"It's too dangerous." Teb studied Marshy's set face. "Think of this—if Kiri and I die there, or are captured, there must be other bards to carry on in our place."

"Camery and Colewolf."

"And if they die in battle . . . ?"

"There is always that chance, wherever we are."

Marshy looked at Teb with a seriousness that made Teb forget how young the child was. "I must go. I might get hurt, Tebriel. But I am a bard. I have as much right as you to go against the dark."

Teb held Marshy's shoulders, looking at him. Marshy's gray eyes stared back, steady and earnest.

"There's something else," Marshy said. "I know something that neither of you know. I know where the slave children are caged."

"How do you know?"

"Hanni made a vision, just for the two of us. We saw the children sleeping in cages."

"And you mean to trade that information for permission to go with us?" Teb shook his head, trying not to smile.

But he knew he didn't, truly, have the right to stop Marshy. One bard did not hold authority over another.

Marshy looked back, waiting.

"Get to bed early," Teb said. "Who knows when we will sleep peacefully again in a safe country."

Marshy hugged him, took a lantern from the table, and went obediently to find an empty bunk. Teb knew that once he was alone, he would speak in his mind to tell Iceflower. When Teb turned from watching him, he saw Gram and Kiri standing in the doorway, framed by an aura of torchlight. He went to them and held Gram in a tight hug. She hugged him back, laughing. Gram had helped him once, risking her own life, when he badly needed help. He felt a special tenderness for her courageous ways. And because she was so dear to Kiri.

The little group had hardly settled before the hearth when the hall doors burst open and three great cats, big as wolves, came bounding in, surrounded by the little owls. Elmmira leaped at Kiri, nearly knocking her down. The pale buff cat pummeled her, growling and licking her face until Kiri doubled up, laughing. When Elmmira backed off to look at her, her long whiskers twitched. "You look fine, Kiri wren. Not too grand after all, even if you do travel with dragons."

Kiri hugged her. "Oh, Elmmira, it's lovely in the sky."

Chocolate-brown Mmenimm snuggled close to Garit, then reared up and began licking his neck. Black Jerymm rolled over before Teb, his great paws waving in the air. But soon the cats settled down, and everyone began asking the bards questions.

Teb and Kiri told them everything that had happened since they left Dacia. When they got to the part about Sivich marching to attack Nightpool, and his soldiers being cut down by Ebis the Black, everyone knew. An owl had brought the news the night of the battle.

Teb said, "Sivich has sent for reinforcements, to attack again. Camery and Colewolf are assembling an army; there are owls on the way to tell you."

"Then why are *you* here, if not to bring the message?" Garit said. "What could be so urgent as to take you away from destroying Sivich and winning back Auric?"

"We have learned that there are two more bard children," Teb said. "Thakkur brought a vision of them. They are held as slaves, in the palace at Aquervell."

The great cats stopped purring. No one moved or spoke.

Teb described the white otters' vision of the drugged children.

"And you are headed for Aquervell," Garit said. "To free them."

The owls were very still. Deep in their round eyes, fear shone. The great cats stared unblinking at Teb and Kiri, their eyes, too, filled with concern.

13

THOSE WHO ENSLAVE OUR NATIONS COME FROM OTHER
WORLDS. WHAT CREATURES MIGHT THEY BRING
THROUGH TO HELP THEM?

———◇———

"What is it?" Teb asked. "What frightens you? We
know there is danger in Aquervell, but you look . . ."
He watched the owls shifting uneasily. And what could
frighten these great cats, who were such courageous
fighters?

Neeno folded his wings close to his body, and looked
back at Teb with round, serious eyes. "Quazelzeg has
brought a monster into Aquervell, from some distant
world."

"Ooo-ooo, something terrible," said his mate, Afeena.
"A monster from beyond the Doors."

"What kind of monster?" Teb said.

"We don't know," said Afeena.

"No one has seen it," said Neeno. "It is locked in a

cave in the old quarry." The little gray owl sat rigid. "Quazelzeg's soldiers have sealed the entrance with boulders. They feed the monster through a hole at the bottom. Oooo, its smell is so vile that even the winged jackals will not go near—though the guard lizards do; they are drawn to the stink. We can hear the monster through the wall of boulders, scrabbling at the stone."

"We can hear it breathe," said Afeena. "We can hear its screams when it feeds. In another cave, behind iron doors, they raise the food for it."

"What is the food?" Teb said.

"They raise rats for it," said Afeena. "Thousands and thousands of huge rats, each as big as six of us. They chase them into barrels and roll the barrels to the creature's cave door. They pull only one stone away, and chase the rats through by banging on the barrel."

"Ooo-ooo, it must be immense," said Neeno, "the number of barrels full of rats it eats."

"When do they feed it?" Kiri asked.

"In the morning," Neeno said. "At first light." The tiny owl walked around Kiri's tea mug and flew to perch on her shoulder. When Elmmira, sitting close to Kiri, lifted her nose to the owl, he rubbed his beak against the tan cat's whiskers.

"Where is the quarry?" Teb said.

Garit took a clay pot from a shelf and poured fine white sand onto the hearth for mapmaking. With a dulled arrow from his quiver, he began to draw the coastline of Aquervell, the city and harbor, the palace north, the old quarry beyond. North of that lay a newer, open quarry, below the mountain where the big fanged lizards lived. At the foot of the mountain was the cave of the monster.

Neeno said, "The monster's cave is perhaps a mile north of the palace. The slave children are caged in the palace courtyard. They are kept mind dulled with cadacus."

Teb nodded. "And it is with cadacus that we will free them."

The owls' eyes widened.

"We will drug the monster," Teb said, "and drug the winged jackals that guard the palace."

"And how will you avoid Quazelzeg's soldiers?" Garit said.

"Let's hope the human ones are sufficiently drugged on their own—and hope all of them are in the middle of their orgies. How many slave children are there?"

"Maybe thirty," said Neeno. "Ooo, maybe more."

"We'll help any way we can," Garit said. "We have plenty of cadacus from King Sardira's stores. We can work it into raw meat for the jackals."

"We'll need a barge," Teb said, "to get the children away. The dragons can't carry so many."

"We'll have a barge," Garit said, "when and where you say. And wagons to meet it."

"Off the tip of Aquervell. From the night we leave until . . . until we meet you."

"How will we drug the monster?" Kiri said.

"We'll drug the rats they feed it," said Teb. "They should like cadacus cakes."

Garit woke three of the ladies who helped in the palace kitchen. They came out yawning, to set about making a paste from flour and water, well laced with the white drug. They spread this out on boards to dry, while the bards prepared drugged meat for the jackals. The next morning, the drugged wafers were cut into squares and packed into two leather bags. It was dawn when they were finished. Musty old clothes had been found for all of them. The owls said the winged jackals sniffed everyone, and that was the smell they were used to.

Neeno chose four owls to fly with him and Afeena, to serve as messengers. The bards could not rely on silent speech, so close to the dark powers.

"The stone gate that closes the palace courtyard is locked at night," Afeena said. "The lock is made of stone. Quazelzeg sleeps with the key on a chain around his throat. The key to the children's cage and their chains hangs somewhere in the palace, perhaps the scullery."

The bards meant to leave Dacia just at dark, to come down over Aquervell late enough so Quazelzeg and his captains would have turned their thoughts to their evening's entertainment. They made two plans, both depending on Neeno and Afeena. If the two bard children were in the outdoor cage, the dragons had only to melt the bars. They would be out of Aquervell within an hour.

If the bard children were not there, the owls would slip into the palace beneath a loose shutter and steal the key, and Marshy would be locked in, chained among the slaves with the key in his pocket. He would wait there until the bard children were returned, then release them. If they were not returned, the plan grew more difficult.

"How do we know there will be extra chains?" Kiri said.

"There are always extra chains," Neeno said. "Many children die there."

As we could die, Kiri thought. She could see the worry in Gram's eyes, but Gram always smiled brightest when she was concerned. The great cats were very quiet as they rubbed against them in a gentle farewell. The cats would leave at dark for Nightpool, to join the other speaking animals in the raid on Sivich.

Garit said, "You promised me once, Tebriel, that I would be with you when you took Auric Palace."

"But I won't be there, either." Teb cuffed Garit's shoulder. "I'll make it up to you. You'll be back in Auric one day, training colts and youngsters there." He hoped nothing happened to Garit, waiting on that lonely barge.

When the bards loaded their bundles onto the dragons' harness, both Seastrider and Windcaller complained that they felt like pack horses. Iceflower and

Marshy remained silent. *They* carried no extra weight, only six small owls who, all together, couldn't weigh a full pound.

The dragons rose into the evening sky, the owls clinging to Marshy's shoulders, their feathers blown back. They stared up with awe at the dragon's huge, beating wings.

A thin moon was beginning to rise; the sky was not yet dark. Before long they could see Aquervell, a wide black smear of land spreading across the pale sea. The wind grew cold. The little owls huddled down inside Marshy's tunic. By the time they reached Aquervell's coast, the sky felt like ice. The harbor lay below, dimly lighted. *When we leave Aquervell*, Teb said, *we'll burn the ships, to keep them from following us*. Beyond the harbor, Quazelzeg's castle rose into the night sky, lit by torches set along the high wall.

Pray that the children are in the cage, Teb said.

I am praying. As they circled, Kiri looked down at the slave cages and the little heaps of blackness huddled inside. The jackals stared up at them from the courtyard and the wall, their wings spread for attack. Teb undid a bag of the drugged meat. As Seastrider dove, he dropped the pieces into the courtyard. The moment the jackals smelled it, they began snarling and fighting over it, their inky shapes thrashing among the shadows. When two jackals flew up at Seastrider, she spit flame at them. They dropped back, but others came. Teb knocked them away. He didn't want to use his sword, and have them dead or wounded for Quazelzeg to see. One grabbed his arm and hung on. He hit it in the face, then pulled its jaws open. It fought him, twisting in the air. He freed his arm and threw the beast down to the pavement, clenching his teeth with the pain of the bite. The owls hissed and dove around him.

"The drug is beginning to work," Afeena said. "They are beginning to stagger."

"Did you find the bard children in the cage?" Teb said.

"No," Neeno said. "We did not."

"Look again. The boy has red hair, the girl is dark."

"Yes, Tebriel. You told us." They dove away, but returned shaking their heads. "We do not think they are there."

Seastrider dove. Teb slipped from her back to the wall, slung his rope over the spikes, and dropped down to the courtyard. In deep shadow, he moved along the cage, looking in. He didn't want to whisper—children trained to drugs could not be trusted. He searched the cage for some time. He could see the children well enough in the torchlight to know the owls were right. The two bards were not there.

Were they in the cellars? He could slip into the palace. There was not a stir of life, no human guard. It would be easy.

Yes, and foolish, Seastrider said. *Your anger must not make you foolish.*

She was right. A foolish risk, with too much at stake. But he burned to go, burned for action, burned with hatred of the dark. He went along the cage again, then swung to Seastrider's back as she lifted straight up with a powerful sweep of wings, to join the others.

Kiri knew Teb's hand was hurting where the jackal had torn it; she could feel the pain making him irritable. She was seared by his impatience that the children weren't in the cage, and by his terrible hatred of the dark. It frightened her to see him so angry—that kind of hatred could lead him into some fatal mistake. And the plan they must now use would put Teb and Marshy alone, among the soldiers of the unliving.

14

IN THE PALACES OF THE DARK, THE UNLIVING RE-
PLENISH THEIR POWERS BY TORTURING THEIR CAP-
TIVES. THEY SUSTAIN THEMSELVES BY BREAKING THE
HUMAN SPIRIT—OH, I PRAY TO THE GRAVEN LIGHT
FOR MY CHILDREN. THE UNLIVING *MUST* BE DRIVEN
FROM TIRROR.

The little owls darted through the moonlight, leading the dragons over a deep, shadowed chasm. Ahead
rose the mountain, its rocky face pale in the moon's
glow and alive with giant lizards oozing over its ledges.
Lizards were crowded at the foot of the mountain, too,
around the wall of mortared stone that sealed the monster's cave. When the dragons dove at them, spitting
flame, the lizards fled.

The dragons settled before the mortared wall, and
the bards slid down and stood looking. The stink of
the monster was like rotten meat. The door at the

111

bottom was just large enough to herd a few rats through. Next to the wall was the cave where the rats were kept—the bards could hear them squeaking and fighting behind the iron door. Two dozen wooden barrels stood waiting to be filled.

"How do they get the monster out?" Kiri said.

Teb examined the wall. "Maybe there's another way, back in the caves."

"Whatever that creature is," Seastrider said, "it is certainly no dragon. No dragon ever smelled like that."

The bards unstrapped the bundles of cadacus wafers from the dragons' harness and began to empty them into the barrels. They sprinkled handfuls of dirt on top, so the wafers wouldn't be seen. The rats would stir them up, seeking the smell of food. As the bards filled the barrels, they could hear stirrings behind the monster's wall, as if the creature was snuffling and scraping along the stone. Suddenly it began to scream. The dragons leaped at the wall, belching flame.

"Get back," Teb shouted. "Do you want to free that thing?" He tried to imagine the shape of the creature, but it touched his thoughts only as writhing darkness. "Come on. Before we all throw up."

Marshy, Kiri, and Teb mounted up, and the dragons leaped skyward, sucking in fresh air.

They circled the highest peak and found a lizard cave. When the giant lizards attacked, the dragons killed them. For over an hour they battled the creatures, pushing the bodies down the mountain into the ravine. The bards swept lizard dung and trash from the cave and laid out their gear. Two pairs of owls went to steal the key to the slave cage and to search for the bard children. Kiri cleaned Teb's arm where the jackal had bitten it; then she put on salve and bound it.

The owls were gone perhaps an hour; then Theeka and her mate swept in on the wind, to drop onto Teb's arm.

"What happened?" Teb said. "Where are Neeno and Afeena?"

"Ooo, on the wall, Tebriel," Theeka said. "Waiting for you. They have the key to the slave cage. It was not in the larder, ooo-ooo, but deep inside the palace, beside the door to Quazelzeg's chambers. Ooo, what a tangled warren of halls."

"Did you find the children?"

"We could hear children," Theeka said. "There were lights in a cellar. Ooo, we heard ugly laughing, and a child screamed. We tried to get in, but there was not a hole big enough. We could see the children through a crack. We could not see the bard children. You will have to use the other plan."

Kiri glanced at Marshy.

Teb laid a hand on the little boy's shoulder. "You can change your mind. No one would think the less of you."

"It will be best if I go right away," Marshy said. "I'm ready—old clothes, musty smell, and all." The little boy squeezed Kiri's hand and climbed onto Iceflower's back.

Teb put on the hooded cloak Garit had given him, like those worn by Quazelzeg disciples. He hugged Kiri and held her. "You have the rope and the rest of the drugged meat. Don't leave here until the owls come for you. It could be a few hours, it could be tomorrow night." He cupped her face in his hands. His look was deep and searching. "It will be all right, Kiri. Be careful . . . for me." His eyes darkened, and he held her to him fiercely. "You . . . it will be all right." He held her tight for a long moment, then turned away as if it were easier to leave her quickly. He leaped to Seastrider's back, Theeka and Keetho swept up to his shoulders, and Seastrider beat up into the night with Iceflower close behind.

Kiri watched dragon and dragonling lift above her and disappear beyond the mountain. She felt lost, torn away from Teb, and she was cold with fear for him. Windcaller stretched out before the cave entrance, watching her. The two owls who had stayed went inside the cave to grub after insects in the rough walls. Kiri stood staring at the empty sky for a long time, trying to be with Teb in her mind. But her vision was stifled by the closeness of the dark. She strained for any sound, and heard nothing. At last she turned back into the cave, drank some water, and lay down with her head on her pack. But her stomach felt empty with terror. Very soon Teb and Marshy would be alone within the walls of the unliving.

Windcaller said, "You were not afraid all those years you spied for Dacia."

"Yes, I was. You didn't know me then. I was afraid for myself, and for Papa."

"Oh," Windcaller said. "But you did your job anyway." She gave Kiri a stern look. "Your fear cannot help Tebriel and Marshy. Only your strength and your cleverness can. You must rest and be ready."

Kiri scowled at Windcaller and closed her eyes, knowing she couldn't rest.

As Seastrider and Iceflower circled above the palace, the only movement in the courtyard was the shadows thrown by the torches, leaping across the still bodies of the jackals. The dragons dropped to the wall, left Teb and Marshy there, and banked away toward the mountain, out of sight.

Teb looped his rope over a spike and went down, his hand never far from his sword. Marshy swung down close behind. They moved toward the slave cage, skirting the drugged jackals. Inside the cage, the children were a dark mass of sleeping bodies huddled close together. Neeno swooped down from the top of the cage and laid the key in Teb's hand. Teb unlocked the gate, and they slipped in, to search, staring into sleeping faces.

They searched for a long time. The two bard children were not there. A dozen chains hung empty. Marshy chose one, and they tried the key to make sure. Yes, the same key unlocked both gate and chains. Marshy locked the steel cuff around his ankle. Teb left him, locked the gate behind him, and passed the key in to Marshy. Marshy hung it on a cord around his neck, underneath his clothes, and settled down in a position of sleep. If he didn't use the key, if they were still there at dawn, Afeena would return the key to the palace before the dark soldiers woke.

Teb followed Afeena's faint flutter as she led him to the outbuilding she had chosen. There, she dropped to his shoulder, to speak softly.

"Neeno and I will be on the roof above you. We will wake you if they bring the children back, or . . . if there is need."

Teb ducked inside and settled down against some barrels, listening for the first stirrings of the jackals. He had an ugly picture in his mind, of a jackal flying up to snatch a little owl from roof or wall. He had not dared drug the creatures enough to leave them asleep when Quazelzeg's soldiers came out at dawn. From his position in the shed he could see part of the courtyard and the slave cage.

He did not mean to sleep. He dreamed of Thakkur, and felt his love powerfully, and then his admonition, *Take care, Tebriel—take care* . . . He woke to a fluttering "Ooo-ooo" that jerked him from sleep with his hand on his sword.

"Shh, Tebriel." Afeena fluttered before him in the graying darkness. "They are coming to take the slaves to the fields. The two bard children were in the cellar! They are being brought up to the courtyard now."

"Did you return the key?"

"I did."

Teb pulled his loose cloak over his sword, moved back among the tools, and knelt beside a wooden plow as if examining the blade. Soon there were footsteps behind him. He heard tools being taken up, men's voices, then, from the yard, the clang of the metal slave gate. Chains rattled, and a voice barked, "Wake up, you filth. Get out of there, get in line."

When there was sufficient commotion in the toolshed, Teb rose, took up half a dozen hoes, and joined the other men. The sky was a flat, heavy gray. The guards were featureless black shadows within their hooded cloaks.

The slave children were marched toward the fields, the limping ones slapped along by the guards. Teb could not see Marshy. The procession was flanked by growling jackals that had come awake irritable and snapping. As it grew lighter, Teb pretended to cuff the children, and he swore at them in a low, angry growl, mimicking the other guards.

On their left lay fields of cadacus plants, waist high and heavy with pods. The sky was growing lighter. But the woods on his right were still thick with shadow. He saw Marshy ahead, stumbling along in a group of children. He searched for the boy with red hair and the dark-haired girl and watched among the trees for the owls. Jackals began to fight among themselves, biting children as well as each other. Suddenly four small shapes winged between the shadowed trees, and

Teb felt easier. If he or Marshy was discovered, it would be only minutes until the owls alerted the dragons. He had no sense of the dragons' voices in his mind, or of Kiri.

As half the children were herded into a field, Teb saw the red-haired boy. The child had stumbled, and a guard kicked him down into the mud, knocking off the dirty cloth he had tied around his head. His hair was red as flame. He had a fresh, bloody wound across his forehead, and his face and arms were bruised. Teb saw Marshy looking, but when a guard paused, Marshy felt Teb's fear and turned back, and began to hoe sullenly. The guard turned away to snap a cadacus pod off a bush, crack it open, and lick the dry fibers inside.

Teb moved ahead, keeping his face down. He looked for the owls but couldn't see them. A lone jackal was winging low in the sky, but he knew the owls wouldn't let themselves be taunted by jackals. He stood slackly, like the guards, seeming to stare at nothing as he searched the ranks of children for the girl. None of the guards paid any attention to him. The two un-men seemed caught between waking and that silent, stony staring the unliving did in place of sleep. The rest seemed simply sullen, or drugged.

Teb couldn't see the girl. Hardly aware he was staring at the red-haired boy, he felt the child touch his mind.

Don't stare at me—turn away! Who are you?

Teb reached to hit at a child near him, turning his

back on the bard child. *I've come to get you out. Where is the girl?*

In the next field. Don't trust her.

But she—

Don't trust her. The boy went silent as, ahead of them, guards began herding some of the children together, teasing them, making them crawl and grovel, then trying to make them lick the cadacus pods. Some children refused, fighting with terror. Others took the drug obediently. When the obedient children groveled, the guards shoved them and laughed. They beat the children who refused the drugs. Teb watched, feeling sick, keeping himself still with a terrible effort. Marshy's silent cry was pleading, *No, Tebriel—don't let them. . . .*

The redheaded boy jerked around to stare at Marshy.

Teb watched, fists clenched. They would risk everything, they would risk the bard children, if they helped.

We can't, *Marshy!*

He tried to meet the redheaded boy's eyes, but the child's face had gone closed and stupid. There was another scuffle, the guards swore, a girl screamed with fury, then voices were lowered. The guards sent the children back to work. Two soldiers started down the lane toward Teb dragging a girl between them.

It was the bard girl, her dark hair tangled around a pale oval face. She was fighting and shouting. "You promised! You promised you wouldn't hurt me!" The soldiers dragged her toward Marshy, jerked Marshy out of the field, and shoved the two toward Teb. At once, he was surrounded by guards, their swords pricking his ribs and throat. When he whistled to signal the owls, a guard hit him across the face.

Marshy shouted, "Neeno . . ." A guard knocked him down. Teb heard an owl scream and saw jackals leaping and feathers on the wind.

Teb's right leg was chained to Marshy's crippled one. They were shoved against a tree as the jackals came to circle them, snapping at their ankles. The girl's legs were chained together. Teb searched the empty sky. *We are captured! Captured!* When a jackal bit him hard, clamping its teeth on his ankle, he kicked it in the face. The guards laughed. They were led away, stumbling in the chains.

Behind them in the cadacus field, the redheaded boy watched their slow, hobbling retreat toward the castle, then returned to hoeing.

15

I HAVE HEARD THAT THE GREATER A MAN'S STRENGTH,
THE MORE PERFECT THE UN-MAN'S PLEASURE IN DE-
STROYING IT. OH, PLEASE, WHATEVER POWERS EXIST
BEYOND US, GUARD MY CHILDREN FROM THE UNLIV-
ING.

Kiri jerked awake, chilled by an owl's scream. She
stared around her. It was light. The owl screamed
again, and she heard the yapping of jackals. She grabbed
her sword and ran scrambling down the mountain toward the cry. The two owls who had been asleep in
the cave swept past her, shouting, "Afeena! Afeena!"
The three dragons dove low over her head.

Halfway down the mountain, among boulders, two
winged jackals were pawing and snuffling at a deep
crack. The dragons dropped on them, belching fire.
Seastrider beheaded one. Windcaller bit the other in
two.

Tybee and Albee hovered over the crack, crying out to Afeena. Kiri knelt and reached in but could barely touch Afeena's feathers. "Come closer. Come to me, Afeena."

Afeena struggled into her hand. Gently, Kiri lifted her out. The little owl's feathers were bloody. Her wings dragged along Kiri's wrist. Kiri carried her up to the cave as Tybee and Albee fluttered around her.

She laid Afeena in her pack among the softest clothes. She was afraid she couldn't examine her gently enough to search for broken bones. One wing drooped out sideways, and Afeena's inner eyelids were half closed. Tybee and Albee huddled into the pack beside her and spread their wings to warm her. Afeena's voice came in a faint whisper.

"Neeno, ooo, Neeno . . . The jackals killed Theeka and Keetho, but Neeno—I helped him into a hole in the tree beside the cadacus field. He is alive—I took him insects, water, in my mouth, but not enough." The little owl coughed, then continued. "The jackals watched me, followed me. He will die—he will starve there. Help him . . ."

"And Teb . . . ?"

"The guards captured them both, in the field . . . the jackals came. . . . Ooo, help Neeno. The tree closest to the lane where the first two fields meet. Neeno . . ."

"Can the jackals get into the hole?"

"No. It is far down and deep. An oak tree."

Kiri tied the remaining bundle of drugged meat to Windcaller's harness and strapped on her pack with Afeena inside. She sent Albee to find Teb and Marshy. She mounted Windcaller carefully, so as not to jar Afeena. Seastrider was in a frenzy to get to Teb, and she knew she must not charge the castle. The three dragons dove for the cadacus field.

Marshy was chained in the slave cage, huddled down, pretending sleep. All the children had been brought in shortly after he and Teb and the bard girl were locked in the cage. The courtyard had been in an uproar, the dark captains arguing, then going quiet and sullen when Quazelzeg appeared. They beat the dark-haired girl and chained her at the far end of the cage.

Marshy watched her, but she wouldn't look at him. What kind of bard was she, to have given away fellow bards? To have ruined her own escape, besides. Across the slave cage, the red-haired boy lay quietly, watching Marshy beneath his crooked arm as he pretended sleep. Marshy had not tried to touch his mind, because the slave girl would know. Fear lay inside Marshy—Teb was somewhere in the palace. He had seen them beat Teb, then march him into the palace in chains. And the dark leader had known Tebriel, had known his name.

They had tried to make Teb say where his dragons were, how many dragons, how many bards. Marshy knew he had to get out of the cage, had to get to Teb.

The tortures would be terrible. Where were the owls? He had to get the key.

The cadacus fields seemed empty as the three dragons skimmed low over the trees. Windcaller came down beside an oak, and Kiri peered into the hole. "Neeno?"

Neeno gave a small, choking answer. Afeena and Tybee slipped in to him. Kiri filled a twist of leather from her waterskin and pushed it into the hole, then crumbled up dried meat and pushed that in, too. Inside, the owls brushed against her hand, helping Neeno. The dragons were fidgeting and nervous.

"Tebriel lies deep in the palace," Seastrider said, trembling. "I can sense him; he is strapped to a table, in a windowless chamber." She shuddered and pawed, huffing fire. "I could storm the palace; I could tear it down. But they would kill him." She looked hard at Kiri. "I will go there into the courtyard, and I will trade myself for him. The unliving would—"

"No!" Kiri stroked the trembling dragon. "That would do no good. They won't give him up, not even to have a dragon. Teb has angered them too often."

"But—"

"We will free him," Kiri said. "Quazelzeg will not kill him. He—he will torture and drug him." That knowledge made her feel sick.

She did what she could for Neeno, but her whole being was shaken with fear for Teb. It took all her strength to make herself wait, with the dragons, deep in the woods until Albee came. The dragons crouched beneath the trees, their wings folded tight, their backs pressed against the low branches, their minds filled with the tortures that battered Teb. The pain of the tortures coursed through Kiri, twisting her, and her mind reeled with the drugs forced into him. When his arms were bent backward, Kiri choked down screams. When Quazelzeg's face filled her mind, and his cold laugh thundered, she fought him just as Teb did. She saw only hazily the false visions with which Quazelzeg filled Teb's mind, but even those images sickened her. The dragons shivered with the power they brought to help Teb. Near to dark, Albee came swooping between branches, rousing them from the horror as he buffeted his wings in their faces.

It was dusk when a kettle of thin gruel was shoved into the slave cage. The stronger children began scooping the slop up in their hands, drinking like starving animals. The weaker ones watched, knowing they would get none, then curled down again to sleep. Marshy shifted position so he could see the red-haired boy, swilling in the gruel. He must speak to him. He must have his help. It would be dark soon; he would go to him then.

But when the children were black silhouettes against the iron bars, most of them asleep, a little wind stirred Marshy, and an owl fluttered close to his face.

"It's Tybee. I have the key."

Tybee dropped onto Marshy's shoulder, and Marshy's hand closed over the cold metal key. He stroked

Tybee, then knelt to unlock his leg chains. He removed them with painful slowness, to make no sound. "They took Tebriel into the palace," he whispered.

"Yes, I found him." Tybee said. "Kiri will go in; she will drug the jackals first. You must unlock all the children, but leave them here. Leave the gate unlocked and closed when you go out. You must help carry Tebriel; he is drugged."

"I will bring the bard boy to help us, too."

Marshy waited for some time after Tybee had gone, watching the still, dark shapes of the children. When no child stirred, he began to crawl, unlocking each child as he went.

It took him half an hour to go the twenty feet to the red-haired boy. Finally he lay beside him, barely breathing. The boy put out his hand, touched Marshy's shoulder, and shifted position so his lips were near Marshy's ear.

"Why have you come?"

"To get you out. You and the girl."

"It was she who told."

"Yes. Why did she?"

"To keep from the things the unliving do to us. She traded the knowledge."

"She is a traitor."

"No, she only lied to help herself. It's worse to be a girl—she is often hurt."

"We mean to get all the children out. What is your name?"

"Aven."

"And hers?"

"Darba."

"Come with me. Do you know the way to Quazelzeg's chambers?"

"Yes."

They waited inside the unlocked gate while Windcaller flew slowly across the courtyard and Kiri dropped the meat. Aven stared up at the white dragon, struck to silence by the sight.

The jackals snatched up the meat, fought, and soon they slept. Windcaller dropped down outside the wall, and Kiri slid onto it. As she secured her rope and swung to the courtyard, Marshy ran to her, dragging Aven. She knelt between them, pulled them close, and told them what she meant to do.

"You can't!" Marshy said. "You can't do that!"

"We must. It is the only way." Kiri hugged him hard. "There is no other way to distract the soldiers. Iceflower agrees. She is very brave, Marshy. And so must you be." She hugged him. "It *will* work. It must work. There are two grown dragons to protect her."

Marshy shook his head, mute and miserable.

Kiri sighed. "We must try it. We must—for Tebriel. We can't wait." She reached into her cloak and gave each boy a knife and sheath. "Strap them on."

She led them along in the shadow of the wall, to the scullery door. "Tybee was able to slide the bolt. It took all his strength."

They slipped through the heavy door into the palace.

16

REBELLION AGAINST THE DARK IS THE GREATEST GIFT
ONE CAN MAKE TO THE GRAVEN LIGHT—IT IS THE
GIFT WE MUST TRY TO GIVE.

———⦿———

Teb lay barely conscious, strapped to a tilting table.
His mouth was bruised and torn; he was covered with
sweat and blood. His drugged mind drifted among lab-
yrinths of terror, and of obedience. Not even when he
had lain for weeks on the drowned seawall, mind tortured by the black hydrus, had he sunk to the depths
he now embraced. Now he loved Quazelzeg with a raw
fear. Quazelzeg was All, was everything, Teb was a
part of him, Teb's will was Quazelzeg's will.

He had no notion that Quazelzeg had left the room,
nor would it have mattered—Quazelzeg was everywhere, his immediate presence only a minute part of
his total presence; his power was in everything.

Teb had no notion that a small gray owl had winged

into the room high against the ceiling shadows, then come to perch on the table to watch him. He would have killed it had he seen it. The floor was scattered with the tools of Quazelzeg's torture and with the metal tubes the dark ruler had used to siphon the drugs into him. Quazelzeg had given him a boiled derivative of cadacus, powerfully intrusive and deforming of the mind.

As Kiri and Marshy approached down the dark passage, a sickening smell made them gag—the same smell as of the caged monster. Could Quazelzeg have brought the monster here? But how, in these small chambers? Soon they stood staring, from the shadows, into the chamber where the smell was strongest.

The room was lit by candles and rich with velvet and gold. Teb was not there, but in the corner stood a small cage. Inside, pressing against the bars, was a little dirty-yellow animal with creased and folded wings and an evil, wrinkled face. They couldn't make out what it was, but its blazing red eyes searched the doorway and the darkness where they hid. When it glanced away, they went on quickly, following Tybee's fluttering shadow. They had left Aven posted down the passage in a storage niche.

They found Teb alone in a bare room, pale, blood-streaked, unconscious. When Kiri untied him and took his shoulders, his head lolled against her. Marshy took his feet, and they fled down the passage and into the storage alcove. His hands and face felt so cold. They hid him behind some crocks and buckets, and Kiri wrapped her cloak around him. His breathing was uneven and thin.

"What did they give him, Aven? Would cadacus make him like this?"

"Boiled cadacus would. They put a metal tube down his throat. See the bruises around his mouth?"

Kiri didn't want to look. She spit on her handkerchief and wiped blood from his face. If his body was so damaged, what scars did his mind hold? "Can we wake him?"

"No, it must wear off."

She took Teb's feet, Marshy and Aven took his shoulders, and they fled past the stinking room of the yellow creature and up the dark stone passages. When they heard the shuffle of boots, they froze against the wall, laid Teb on the floor, and waited, knives and sword drawn.

Two human warriors went by along the cross passage, never looking to right or left, walking with the rigid, unbalanced gait of the drugged.

The bards were almost to the scullery when a shout sent them running and stumbling. They pushed Teb beneath a scullery table and crouched, weapons drawn, as footsteps pounded toward them.

"Albee . . ." Kiri breathed. "Albee . . ."

"Ooo—here." The owl dropped onto her wrist.

"Tell Iceflower—tell her, *Now!*"

The little owl fled, winging through the scullery and

out through a crack above the shutter. Feet pounded by them, and more toward the main door, some so close Kiri could have tripped the dark soldiers. Suddenly a dragon's scream filled the palace, echoing from the courtyard, and confused shouting began—Iceflower had begun her act. Kiri slipped to the scullery door to look.

The courtyard was aflame with Iceflower's breath. She was rearing, dodging swords, screaming—she twisted away from soldiers who leaped at her head, trying to throw ropes over her. All attention was on the dragonling. Kiri grabbed Teb's legs; they pulled him from under the table, fled into the shadows of the courtyard, and ran stumbling along the dark wall. They made for the blackest corner, nearly knocked down by milling soldiers backing away from Iceflower. Behind them, Quazelzeg had appeared in the main doorway, shouting, "Get the nets—get the nets on it!" Kiri was terrified he would see them.

Suddenly white fury dropped out of the sky as Seastrider dove, spitting flame, crushing soldiers. She banked to Kiri, took Teb in her mouth, and shoved him onto her back. Marshy climbed up to tuck Teb's legs into the harness. In the center of the yard, Iceflower knocked chains away and melted them, burning soldiers—but a captain saw Teb.

"The bard's escaping! Get the bard!" The soldiers abandoned Iceflower and charged Seastrider.

"No!" Quazelzeg roared. "Forget the bard! The bard

is mine now! Catch the dragon—*I want the dragon!*"

As the dark soldiers turned back to circle Iceflower, Seastrider lifted clear. Kiri grabbed Aven's hand, and they ran for the slave cage. "The girl first," Kiri said. "Get the girl!"

Windcaller dropped down out of the sky to them as the slave children swarmed around the gate. When Kiri flung the gate open, she saw the bard girl. The bolder children surged out, and the bard girl's eyes met Kiri's. She was pressing forward three timid, confused children, but they fought her, backing and staring. Aven moved to help her, and together they herded the children toward Windcaller, pushing and dragging.

"Don't be afraid," the bard girl begged. "It's a singing dragon! She'll free us." But the three children balked and turned back.

"She won't *hurt* you!" Kiri cried. "She'll carry you to safety. Go to her!" She lifted one and pushed him up onto Windcaller. "She's a singing dragon, she won't hurt you!"

They got ten of the boldest onto Windcaller's back, Aven and the bard girl pushing the last ones up as the big dragon lifted. In the center of the courtyard, Iceflower was bleeding badly but she thrashed and roared, teasing and distracting the soldiers.

Seastrider returned and Marshy slid down, panting, "Tebriel is safe on the barge." As they pushed children onto Seastrider's back, they saw soldiers poised on the wall above Iceflower, spreading a net.

132

"Heave . . ."

"*Now!*"

The net fell over the fighting young dragon in pale folds.

"Tighter—pull it tighter!"

Iceflower plunged and flamed, burning net, burning soldiers, as Windcaller returned.

It was all Kiri and Aven and the girl could do to get the last children mounted. Where was Marshy? Then Kiri saw him in the center of the courtyard, clinging to Iceflower, both of them tangled in the net. Kiri swung onto Windcaller's back behind a tangle of children, and Windcaller sped at the soldiers, blasting flame. Seastrider, loaded with children, dropped to fight beside her.

The dragons cut the net away, Marshy scrambled onto Iceflower's back, and the three dragons lifted, Iceflower limping in flight, the big dragons heavy and slow with the weight of the children. They made for the cadacus field as soldiers with torches stormed out the gate.

While Seastrider and Iceflower circled, Windcaller dropped to the oak, and Kiri reached in. "Quickly, come on. Neeno, Afeena. Hurry."

Tybee and Albee swept out to her shoulder. Afeena and Neeno crept into her hand as torches appeared, coming fast. She tucked the two owls into her tunic. The dragons pulled for the sky, fighting to lift themselves above the treetops.

133

High up in cloud, Kiri felt the child behind her relax against her. The pounding of her own heart eased. She felt like screaming with relief. She looked across at Iceflower. The poor dragonling was fighting the wind instead of using it, breeching across it in weak, uneven struggle. *It won't be long,* Kiri said. *It isn't far to the barge. You were very brave—you did a fine job, both of you.*

She could feel Marshy's pride in the dragonling and his shivering relief that they were out of there. She could feel Aven's wonder as the little boy looked down through the night sky. Now that they were away, the bard girl seemed strangely remote. They were just over the lights of Lashtel's harbor when Kiri remembered what Teb had intended to do. "Drop!" she cried. "Circle, drop down!"

17

THE UNLIVING CONQUER BY CHANGING ALL MEMORY AND NAMING THEMSELVES OUR SAVIORS. ONLY THE BARDSONG CAN DESTROY THEIR LIES, AND WITHOUT DRAGONS, THE BARDSONG IS ALL BUT GONE FROM TIR-ROR.

———◦∞◦———

"The ships," Kiri cried. "Burn the ships!"

The dragons dropped with their burden of children, and skimmed low over Aquervell's seaport, driving a wind before them that rocked the tethered boats. They belched out sheets of fire—a ship blazed up, another. Dry decks and masts exploded into flame. Soon the whole harbor was burning. In the pulsing red glare, men dove into the water or ran along the quays, screaming. From the backs of the dragons, the children watched wide-eyed. While the harbor roared and crackled with flame, the dragons rose into the smoky wind and headed for the tip of Aquervell.

The late moon hung behind cloud, the sea black shadows cresting and moving—every shadow might be the barge, they couldn't see it clearly until they were nearly on it. Seastrider breathed a small flame, and they saw it rocking below them. In the red light, they saw Garit and the children crouched beside the still body of Tebriel. Two rebel soldiers stood guard. The dragons came down on the sea.

Children slid to the deck, the soldiers catching the smallest ones. Seastrider nuzzled at Teb. Kiri slid down, to kneel beside him.

He was unconscious, his face cold and white, smeared with dark bruises. Garit had covered him with a pile of blankets. Kiri looked up at Garit, helpless and afraid. "He hasn't moved, or spoken?" Garit shook his head. Kiri held Teb's hands, trying to warm them. What could she do for him? How could she help him?

Desperate, she began to talk to him—maybe the sound of a voice would touch something in him. Maybe a voice could be a lifeline of human warmth, to draw him back. She told him they had gotten the children out, that they now had two new young bards, that the dragons all were safe. She told him how Iceflower had kept the soldiers busy while they carried him out of the castle, how they got the children onto the dragons. She told him that they had burned the harbor. Teb showed no sign that he heard, and Quazelzeg's words rang cold in her mind. *The bard is mine now.*

Stricken, she kept talking—it didn't matter what

she said; all that mattered was that she connect with what was alive deep within him. Somewhere within his wounded mind he *must* hear, something of his spirit *must* hear her. She paid no attention to the bustle around her as the men set sail. As they sloughed through the surf, she talked about Nightpool, about the otters, about Charkky and Mikk, about how Thakkur and Hanni had been so excited to find each other. The slave children listened, entranced. As the moon dropped below clouds, Kiri could see the children's faces, hungry for story, hungry for life and warmth. She could feel Seastrider's smooth summoning of Tebriel, too, as the dragon sought to pull him back from emptiness with silent power. As the barge moved across open sea, Kiri spoke of the magic places, of the sacred sanctuaries, and how men and speaking animals had once found fellowship there. She could see the wonder and longing on the faces of the slave children.

They were nearly past Ekthuma, the night fading. Teb's eyelids moved. When Kiri felt his cheek, it was warmer. She told him again that they had escaped from Quazelzeg, that the children were safe. Garit poured tea from the crock—he had given the children tea and bread and cheese. Kiri brushed the warm tea across Teb's lips, and after a long time, when he licked his upper lip, she felt like cheering.

"Lift him, Garit. Help me lift him, to lean against the mast."

When he was sitting up, she put the mug to his lips.

He swallowed. The cup shook in her hand. Seastrider pushed at him and licked his face. He was alive; he had come back to them.

But there was no recognition in him. He sat staring at them blankly, his body awake but his mind not yet returned. Seastrider nudged and worried at him. Then, frustrated, the white dragon began to sing to him, forming lucid visions of moments she and Teb had shared.

As the raft made its way south toward Dacia, Seastrider's song took them across the shifting endless skies, buffeted by twisting winds, soaring on thrones of rain and swirling ice. She lifted them above islands of dark clouds humping like the backs of a million giant animals, and over cloud plains white as snowfields. She dodged lightning through crashing black storm, and she sang of silent lands like green jewels, where rivers ran in a tracery of blue.

The slave children drank in the splendid wonders, hugging to themselves hungrily all Seastrider's wild freedom and fierce love. But Teb sat quiet and pale, staring at his hands, seeming aware of nothing. Seastrider pressed her big white head against him, and Kiri held him close, but he did not respond to them.

When an agitated rustling began in Kiri's pack, she opened it, and little injured Neeno crawled up out of the darkness, his wings dragging. The tiny owl stood tottering on the leather strap, staring at Teb, his round yellow eyes deep with puzzled concern. "He is very ill." Neeno blinked, clacked his curved beak in a loud staccato, and shouted with all his remaining strength, *"Wake, Tebriel! Ooo, wake!"* He peered at Teb. *"Do you hear me? Wake!"* He cocked his head, looking. *"Oooo! Wake, Tebriel! Wake! Wake!"* He clattered again, and his angry shout rose to a commanding shriek. *"Bring yourself back, Tebriel! Wake up, Tebriel! Wake up!*

"DARE you wake, Tebriel? DARE YOU? Are you afraid to wake?"

Teb stirred and looked at Neeno. That angry, clacking shout had brought him back. Perhaps it was like the angry, chittering sound an otter makes; perhaps it made Teb think of Mitta commanding him to get well. He reached to touch Seastrider as she nuzzled him, he touched Kiri's cheek. He looked at the crowd of children, at Marshy, at Aven and Darba and Garit and the two rebel soldiers.

He frowned at the little owl's bloody, twisted wings and held out his hand for Neeno to climb on. "What happened? Where are the others?"

Albee and Tybee and Afeena came swooping from the top of the mast and crowded onto Teb's shoulder.

"Theeka? Keetho?"

"They were killed," Kiri said. "The jackals . . ."

Teb touched Neeno's bloody feathers and held the little owl to his cheek, his eyes filled with sorrow. Neeno closed his own eyes and snuggled against Teb.

As they neared the coast of Dacia, Teb told them a

little about Quazelzeg's torture. His cheeks burned with shame that he had been so used. He did not speak of the abyss where his every human need had been a sickness, but Kiri knew, she and the dragons knew. For those terrible hours, they had felt Quazelzeg owning him. Kiri moved within Teb's encircling arm, and he held her close. The slave children pressed against them in a warm wall of small bodies.

Only Aven stood apart. His rusty brown eyes had changed suddenly and grown dark with excitement.

"What is it?" Kiri said.

"There are four dragonlings in Dacia," Aven said.

"Yes," Teb said. A smile twitched the side of his mouth.

"One is blue," said Aven.

"Yes!" Teb and Kiri cried together. The dragons' eyes gleamed.

"He has named himself Bluepiper," Aven said, "after a snowbird from across the western sea."

Teb laughed out loud—the first time he had laughed—and hugged Aven.

Darba pressed against Aven. "You . . . you have found your dragon." Excitement filled her dark eyes, but beneath that excitement were shadows of loneliness. Kiri drew the little girl to her. She studied Darba's heart-shaped face and dark, tangled hair, then dug into a pocket of her tunic and took out her small shell comb.

She combed Darba's hair as gently as she could,

taking her time, working out the tangles, humming to Darba. The questions Aven was asking about Bluepiper, and Teb's exciting answers, came easier for the little girl when she was stroked and loved. By the time Garit put ashore at Dacia, Aven knew almost everything about Bluepiper and the clutch of young dragons. And Darba's longing jealousy had eased. Kiri tied the child's shining hair back with a bit of white leather. "You are lovely, do you know that? Some decent food, and you'll feel better, too." She drew Marshy to her, so the three of them stood close.

"Take Darba to the palace with you, Marshy. Iceflower's wounds will be all right; she's bathed them in the sea, and she's rested. She'll be strong enough for the two of you for that short distance."

Marshy put a protecting arm around Darba. "Come on," he said. "Iceflower will take us home." He gave Darba a leg up onto Iceflower's back and climbed up behind. As dawn touched the sky over Dacia, Iceflower lifted carefully into the wind and headed for the palace.

18

I WATCH THE SKY FOR DRAGONS THAT WILL NEVER
COME. MY KING KNOWS MY PAIN; HE KNOWS THAT
TIRROR IS DYING. HE KNOWS THE EMPTY FACES OF
THE YOUNG.

———◦◦◦———

Garit and the two soldiers bent heavily to the oars,
pushing the raft through shallow surf toward Dacia's
wooded shore. As Kiri leaped to the bank to make fast
the line, the dark branches above her shivered and a
big winged shadow burst out, to dive straight at her.
She ducked, laughing, as the big owl flashed dark,
gleaming feathers in her face. "Red Unat!" She held
out her arms, and Red Unat dropped into them so
powerfully he nearly knocked her over. He clacked his
red beak, and shook his big ears. His yellow eyes blazed
fiercely. His manners were as abrupt and crusty as
ever. But he was a true friend—a skilled spy and
messenger for the underground. She and Papa had

worked with him here in Dacia, and Teb had known him in Nightpool. The big owl snapped his beak again. His voice was coarse and gravelly. "About time! About time you got here! Tired of waiting! Thought that dark continent swallowed the lot of you."

"It almost did," Kiri said, stroking his dark, sleek wing.

"The wagons are waiting," Red Unat said. "Hitching up now, to take the children." As he looked up at the sky, now growing bright, the pupils of his eyes narrowed to slits.

Teb stood up, leaning on Garit's shoulder. "Red Unat! What brings you? Has Sivich attacked Nightpool?"

Red Unat shook his feathers. "Sivich's warriors gather for attack. Every traitor the dark can muster is camped at the Palace of Auric." He stared at Teb. "You look terrible—all scars and bruises. I'm glad to see you are alive, Tebriel."

"So am I," Teb said. "What is Sivich's plan of attack?"

"He means to destroy Nightpool just at dawn, then go straight up the coast to burn Ebis's palace. He waits only for additional troops." Red Unat smiled, a wicked smile. "Sivich doesn't know the otters sank his courier boat, so his plea for troops didn't get through." He clacked his beak in an owlish laugh. "He's furious at being tricked by animals, his horses taken, half his supplies gone, half his soldiers dead. Our owls have spy holes in every nook and attic of the palace; we hear everything." The big owl stretched his wings, then snapped them closed. "But we cannot be over-confident. Sivich is a pawn of the dark powers—they will not let him lose so easily again." He looked around the little group. "Another owl will come when Sivich is ready to move. Tell me what word has reached the dark leaders at Aquervell."

"We don't know," Teb said. "We . . . were lucky to get out of there."

"That I can see. Well, no matter. I have sent owls on, to Quazelzeg's palace, to find out. Let's get these children onto the wagons. Did you get the bard children out?"

"The girl has gone on, with Marshy," Teb said. "The boy is here." He drew Aven to him.

Red Unat stared at Aven. "Fine boy!" he shouted. "Hair as red as my beak!"

Aven blushed.

"We lost two brave owls," Teb said. "The jackals killed Theeka and Keetho."

Red Unat's feathers bristled. His glare was terrible.

"Neeno and Afeena are badly hurt," Teb said. "They're in Kiri's pack, warm and as comfortable as she could make them."

The big owl poked his face at Kiri's pack and murmured to the small owls. He remained talking to them until the wagons came rumbling out of the woods.

The children were bundled in among blankets. Teb and Kiri rode with them, while Seastrider and Windcaller swept off toward open sea to feed.

By the time they reached the palace, Kiri could think of nothing but food. She took Teb's hand, and they headed for the kitchen. Garit carried the little owls into his chamber to doctor them, calling for raw meat. Red Unat rode on his shoulder, giving instructions.

In the kitchen, two townswomen were frying wheat cakes and lamb. They shouted when they saw Kiri, and hugged her. Both had fought beside her. The younger woman was a crack shot with bow and arrow, the thin, older lady had run the candle shop where the resistance hid weapons and food. Kiri kissed them and stood with Teb at the stove, eating as fast as they served up the food, blowing on each piece of lamb or wheat cake as it came out of the pan. Nothing in her life had ever tasted so wonderful. There was all the milk they could drink, and all the bread and cheese and fresh fruit they wanted. It took her a long time to get filled up, much longer than Teb. He soon pushed his plate away, looking tired and pale.

They stayed in the bustle of the kitchen, at the big table, as platters were carried out to the hall for the children. Teb was morose and silent.

"It's all over, Teb. We did it—we got the children out."

He didn't say anything.

"It's over, Teb."

"I should have fought Quazelzeg harder. I . . . kept dropping into blackness, where I thought there was nothing to fight against. I—I *wanted* to belong to him, Kiri."

"I know. The dragons and I sensed your battle."

His eyes searched hers, sick at what she had seen.

She took his hand in both of hers. "I'm glad I was with you." She tried to see his strength, see the old rebelliousness in his eyes, but she didn't quite find either.

When they left the kitchen at last, to look for Marshy and the bard children, Kiri felt cold and disturbed. They found Marshy and Darba tucked up in bunks, under linen sheets and warm blankets, sound asleep. Aven lay awake, too filled with thoughts of Bluepiper to sleep.

"When will I see him? When will we be on Windthorst?"

"Soon," Kiri said. "Very soon." She straightened his covers and hugged him. They stayed with him, talking softly, until he drifted off. When they returned to the great hall, the children were still feasting, whispering softly, still too unused to their freedom to be loud and natural. Kiri wanted to gather them all in and care for them.

When she sat on the raised hearth, beside Teb, a thought kept nagging at her, that Teb might be much harder to heal than she had thought. She pushed the idea away. When she looked up, a big owl was hovering in the sun-filled doorway.

It was a brown barn owl with a face like a mask, its eyes squinting in the sunlight. When it did not see Red Unat, it dove straight to Teb.

146

He was smaller than Red Unat, but bigger than the little gray owls, brown as chocolate, with a creamy face. His voice was as deep as a drum.

"Sivich will attack tonight. He will ride straight for Nightpool."

Teb sat up straighter, studying the owl.

The owl said, "Sivich was overheard to say he intends to sleep in the bed of Ebis the Black tonight—after a supper of roast otter."

"He'll burn in hell first," Teb said.

"His armies wait for darkness, in the caves north of Auric." The owl smiled a fierce hunter's smile. "At nightfall, Camery's troops will gather on the high ridge above them—where they can come down on Sivich like an owl on a tangle of mice."

Teb laughed. "And we will be there. We will leave Dacia two hours before dusk, to arrive on the ridge just after dark has fallen."

Kiri felt her heart ease with the return of Tebriel's sure, uncomplicated strength.

"I will take the message," the owl boomed. He swooped to the breakfast table, gulped down half a plate of lamb and wheat cakes, and with one wink at Teb, sped out the door, for Auric.

It was later, as Kiri and Teb knelt on the floor of the hall cutting out harnesses for Bluepiper and for one other young dragon, that she said, yawning, "I need sleep badly. So do you." When she looked up, she was amazed at the anger in his eyes.

147

"What did I say?"

"I don't need sleep. Don't nag me."

"I'm not nagging! Of course you need sleep!" She stared at him, crushed. He stared back, furious, but she saw pain deep beneath his anger, and saw confusion at his own temper. Yet when she reached to put her arms around him, he scowled and turned away, his thoughts closed to her. With a final angry glare he rose and left the hall.

She knelt there, staring after him, then followed. But halfway to the door she stopped and stood watching his retreating back. Then she spun around and ran—across the sunlit hall past the staring children, and out into the courtyard and across it. . . .

She burst into the cottage, startling Gram at the cookstove, and threw her arms around her.

When she was done crying, Gram sat her down and gave her tea and fresh bread spread with butter and honey. After finding Kiri a handkerchief, Gram said, "It was bound to happen. Be glad he is a bard."

"What are you talking about?"

"You wouldn't want to be in love with an ordinary man. Your father loved an ordinary woman. Life was hard for them. Teb's mother loved an ordinary man. A king, but ordinary, not a bard. It must have been terrible for him when she left. You love a bard. Be glad."

Kiri stared at Gram. Love had nothing to do with this; she was only concerned for Teb, frightened at the change in him, hurting at the terrible thing that had happened to him. She shivered and buried her face against Gram's shoulder, uncertain how she felt.

"It will be all right, Kiri."

"He's so angry, Gram. So . . . different." She didn't want to say weakened. She didn't want to say possessed, or remember Quazelzeg's words . . . *The bard is mine now.* . . .

Gram held her and didn't say anything, and after a while she was telling Gram all that had happened in Aquervell, all the terror of Quazelzeg's terrifying invasion of Teb's mind.

When she had finished, Gram held her close while she cried again. She had never been one for hysterics. What was the matter with her?

"Tebriel needs rest, Kiri. Let him be awhile."

Kiri shivered.

Gram held her away, looking hard at her. "Give Tebriel your faith. And your trust. He is still Tebriel! He fought beside you to save Dacia. He bled in the arena, nearly died there. Oh, Kiri, the terrible twisting of his mind, the pain, the drugs—it will take time for him to heal, but he *will* heal. Give him time."

She looked steadily at Gram. "We leave for Windthorst two hours before dusk. To fight Sivich and the dark armies."

Gram's look went naked with fear. Then she smiled. "Tebriel will be strong. He will be strong, Kiri! And you will be strong, with him. Now, come, you need rest."

Gram bedded her down on fresh sheets, near the

wood fire. "Sleep for a little while. I will wake you in midafternoon." She kissed Kiri, looking deep into her eyes, and left her.

But Kiri didn't sleep. She lay awake thinking thoughts that would not let her sleep.

19

THERE ARE MANY EVILS BEYOND THE DOORS THAT
COULD DESTROY ME. BUT TO GIVE IN TO MY FEAR
WOULD DESTROY ME WITHOUT QUESTION.

———✺———

When the dragons had fled Quazelzeg's palace courtyard, the dark leader stood cold with rage that a dragonling had been so nearly captured, then lost. He
swore at his inept captains and watched impatiently
as the stronger officers tried to strike order.

As officers and troops came to attention, all eyes
focused on him. He looked them over, searing his gaze
into them until the humans among them flinched.

"You have lost the dragon. You have lost the slaves
and the bard children with your clumsiness." He paused,
letting them sweat. No eye dared blink, no hand move.

"You have failed the leaders whom you serve!"

He did not mention Tebriel's escape. He would have
freed Tebriel anyway. The Prince of Auric was his

now; Prince Tebriel would do his work now. Quazelzeg smiled. Now, Tebriel himself would help him recapture the bard children and help him snare the dragonling—whether willingly or unknowingly didn't matter. No distance, now, could destroy his hold over the bard prince.

How interesting the way these things worked out. He had no notion how Tebriel had found out about the captive bard children, but on balance, Quazelzeg knew the dark had gained more than it had lost.

Still, he must have the child bards back. And he would have the dragonling with them.

"Mechek, Igglen, you will take forty men, ready a ship, and go after the bards. You will return to me only when you have the two bard children—*and* the dragonling."

The officers dared not speak.

"I will use my powers to help you," he said with studied softness. "I will see that Tebriel himself leads you to those you are to capture."

The officers stared.

"Go on! Get to Lashtel! What are you waiting for! Go and ready a ship, to follow the dragons! They will head either for Dacia or for Windth—"

Suddenly the courtyard was gone.

He stood alone in a dark mist.

There was no sound. He shielded himself with power. What trick was this?

A black Door shone before him, cut sharply out of

the mist, a heavy Door strapped and hinged with iron. As he looked, it grew taller until it rose as high as his castle towers. When it swung inward, he stood scowling into the deeper darkness beyond. Such a trick could not last long—no one had the power to deceive him for long. He raised his hand to wipe the vision away, but a woman appeared in the doorway, and her presence held him still.

She was tall and tawny haired. Her green eyes shone with an intense, disturbing power. He willed her away from him, yet he was drawn to her. A white dragon slipped out of the blackness to rear and coil around her, spreading its wings above her. It stared down at him with eyes like hers, eyes of green fire. Its tongue came out and curled and licked as if it would like to snatch him up and swallow him.

The woman's voice was soft. "You are Quazelzeg." She smiled, but not a soft smile. He was staring at her, deciding which power to use to banish her, when he saw Sharden lying below, as if he stood on a mountain. Sharden—*his* city, where lay his second castle. He could see his disciples and slaves down there; the woman and dragon were there, as well as here before him. There were other dragons winging above the castle.

What did this mean?

A voice riveted him. Not the woman's voice but the dragon's, deep and thunderous:

"I am *the* dragon, Quazelzeg. *I* am the one you must

seek." The dragon smiled, bloody mouth gaping, white teeth like blades, flames spurting from deep within. Quazelzeg stared, hating it—and lusting to own it.

"*I* am the one you must follow," it said. "If you follow me—and if you can kill me—you will win this world completely.

"But only by killing me. *Only me . . .*"

The dragon turned. The woman looked at Quazelzeg for a moment, calmly, in full command. Her eyes held a deep challenge that infuriated him. When she turned, she swung onto the dragon's back; it spun, and they were gone into blackness.

He stood staring after them. Countless Doors began to appear, opening into uncounted worlds. He could see the dragon racing through, so that it seemed to be a thousand dragons. Wherever he looked, Doors shone in a spinning tangle of chambers and caves and infinite space, and always the dragon was racing through as if it challenged him to follow.

He did not want to admit that this was more than trickery. He could turn and go back to his own palace— or he could follow and destroy them. He stood for an instant alone between worlds, lusting with the challenge. Then he brought his powers around him like protecting armor and stepped into the careening blackness.

The two white dragons beat across a powerful wind, easing a path for Iceflower, who limped along behind them. It was just dusk. Aven rode before Teb, filled with eager visions of a blue dragonling. Darba rode in front of Kiri, her wonder touching Kiri powerfully: She was free; she was with other bards like herself. She was, ultimately and joyously, with dragons. Kiri hugged the little girl and smiled.

Yet when Kiri looked across at Teb, that hurtful unease crawled in her mind again. She tried to hide her uncertainty. When he touched her thoughts with a powerful sense of needing her, she responded with all her strength. In the thin moonlight, his look was so honest, and so caring, that she reached through space to touch his hand between sweeps of the dragons' wings.

Ahead of them, on Windthorst, Camery and Cole-wolf's armies waited in silence atop the mountain ridge above Sivich's camp. Many of the warriors who waited with them had, a day ago, been slaves of the unliving. Awakened to the visions of dragon song, these men and women and children had armed themselves and made their way south, side by side with the speaking animals.

Owl spies patrolled mountain and valley, winging silently through the night between Camery's camp and Ebis's army, waiting on the ridge farther north.

Ebis lounged beside his black stallion, letting the animal graze at the sparse grass. He was a big man, broad of shoulder and with a heavy, curling black beard. Not since he had won Ratnisbon back, some years ago, had a battle excited him so. This night's work must make an end to Sivich—and a beginning to the end of the dark rulers. Certainly the dragonbards had fanned the fires of revolt across the larger continents to a roaring blaze. Many slaves had turned on their masters and killed them, and joined with Camery's troops.

Thinking of Camery made him smile. He remembered her as a little girl. She had grown up very like her mother—a fighter just like Meriden. A fine figure she made on that black dragon, a daughter Meriden would be proud of. He made a fervent warrior's prayer for her in this battle; and for Tebriel and his bards to return safely from Aquervell.

Quazelzeg followed the woman and dragon through endless Doors, planning to drive them into some dark world where he could destroy them. He could hear the deathly cries of the soulless multitudes, very near. Soon he was moving through a mass of writhing cadavers, thinking how best to draw the woman and dragon to him. The creatures clustered around him, reaching up. Moldering bodies cried out to him. He trampled and kicked them, taking pleasure and strength from their pain, knowing they would take the same from him if they could—but knowing they could suck life from the dragon. As he strode across the bodies, hurrying after the dragon, the creatures' bloody hands began to pull at him. He beat them back, but they clutched and heaved, climbing up him until suddenly he was no longer taking power from them—they were taking power from him. He ran, turning back to strike at them.

He saw the dragon very near. It was smiling; the woman, Meriden, was smiling. He swung at the bodies with fury. They clung, covering him. He fell under their weight, was smothering under creatures that sucked at his power to build *their* strength. He screamed. . . .

The bodies vanished; the dragon was gone, the woman gone. He stood in his own courtyard, staring at the flickering torchlight. He was alone, and it was night, not morning. The thin moon was low overhead. There was no soldier in the courtyard, no servant. He shouted for officers and servants. How long had he been away? How long . . . ?

His captains came running, the humans among them stumbling and bleary eyed. Captain Vighert cowered before him, his face white.

"We thought you dead," Vighert said. "You fell, in the courtyard. We carried you to your chambers—you lay as if dead. . . ."

"I am not in my chambers. I am not dead. Have you sent for ships?"

"There are no ships," Vighert said. "They burned the ships."

The officers watched, the un-men without expression.

"There are no ships," Vighert repeated.

"Did you open the cave? Did you release the queen?"

"We . . . no. You gave no such order."

Quazelzeg stared at Vighert, then up at the darkening sky. "How long . . . ?"

"Since this morning," Vighert said.

"Why didn't you open the cave?"

"You gave no such order."

"Open it now. And go to my chamber, Vighert, and bring the queen to me." He smiled. "If my pets kill the entire lot of bards and dragons, so be it. If they do not . . ." His smile deepened to a white scar of stretching mouth. "If they do not, what is left will come crawling to me for protection."

"But how can they follow? There is no scent—we don't know . . ."

"They will follow. Open the cave."

Vighert stared.

Quazelzeg said patiently, "It will be Tebriel himself who will lead my pets to the dragons." Yes, Meriden's son would lead them, and that would be the sweetest revenge of all. He looked at his hands, which he kept immaculate, and saw filth from endless worlds.

By the time the creatures were released, the thin moon was dropping into the west. Quazelzeg's pets swept out through the hole at the bottom of the wall, up into the night, following their queen, their wings cutting the wind with a dry, snapping sound, their little sharp teeth gleaming, their little dull minds dreaming of blood. Their yellow queen led them with sporadic shiftings across the sky, pulled by a thin, uncertain beckoning. The black cloud of vamvipers shifted with her, changing and changing shape like black smoke, filling the wind with their stink.

It was just dark when Camery looked up suddenly to see three smears of white moving fast across the stars. "Teb," she breathed. She stifled a shout of greeting as the white dragons slipped across the wind and dropped for the mountain. The massed warriors moved back to give them room, and the three came to rest in a furling of wings. Camery could feel Kiri's silent cry, *Papa! Oh, Papa!*

Starpounder and Nightraider reared, nudging their sisters in greeting, fanning their wings over them, nearly smothering the bards. Kiri slid down and ran into Colewolf's arms, and clung close. The three dragonlings came dropping out of the sky, where they had been patrolling, to press around Iceflower, nudging and caressing her. Only Rockdrumlin was missing, as he carried Charkky and Mikk over Auric Palace.

Camery hugged Teb and held him, then pulled Marshy to her. She saw the two new children and reached to gather them in, but the red-haired boy moved away from her and stood alone, staring at Bluepiper.

As the dragonling stared at the boy, all whispering stopped.

Child and dragonling looked at each other for a long time, with the troops so still around them that Camery could hear Aven swallow. Suddenly Bluepiper snorted softly, bowed his neck, and pushed his face down at Aven. The little boy wrapped his arms around the dragonling's blue, scaly nose. They remained so until Aven flung himself onto the dragonling's back and leaned over, hugging Bluepiper and gulping back tears.

When he slipped down from Bluepiper's back, it was to buckle on the harness Teb and Kiri had made. Quickly he mounted again, and Bluepiper leaped for the sky. Darba watched them with envy.

Kiri put her arm around Darba and drew her close. "I have no dragon, either," she said. Darba looked up, her eyes wide with surprise.

"Nor has Windcaller a bard," Kiri said. "Windcaller and I travel together, but we are not paired. You will travel with one of the dragonlings until you find your own dragon mate."

The little girl looked incredulous; then joy spilled out in a bright smile. She grabbed Kiri, hugging wildly, her excitement sweeping them both. Kiri held her tight, and over Darba's shoulder she saw Firemont looking. She beckoned to him.

The red-black dragonling came nuzzling, pushing at Darba with a sly look in his eye. Kiri showed Darba how to harness him. He sighed with pleasure as the little girl buckled on the soft leather. "You are beautiful," Darba whispered.

"And you are the most beautiful of all possible girl children," Firemont answered.

As Kiri gave the child a leg up, Firemont opened his wings and lifted away silently into the night. Soon they were lost in the blackness.

Teb had watched the child and dragonling—a stupid display of sentiment. He walked away by himself and stood looking morosely down the cliff where Sivich's armies were hidden.

The moon shone across the top of the ridge, but it would leave Camery's descent down the mountain in blackness. She had planned very well, he admitted crossly.

He was confused and puzzled by his own anger. Something was pulling at him, and had been ever since he had left Aquervell. He reached out to face it, irritated and very tired. He felt it quicken, and felt his interest in it quicken.

Kiri watched Teb, frowning, but when she went to join him, he moved away from her along the mountain rim. She stood staring after him, then turned away and went to stand with Papa. Colewolf put his arm around her. They stood looking down the cliff, where they could hear the occasional jingle of a halter chain and a muffled voice.

It was bad, in Aquervell, Colewolf said. *Very bad for Tebriel.*

Yes. Very bad.

You're afraid for him.

She showed him what had happened to Teb.

He squeezed her shoulder, held her close. His solid

warmth and his silent, reassuring thoughts strengthened her. Her father had great power. His silence—
the muteness of his voice and the quiet of his nature—
was deceptive. They stood for a long time, his spirit
firm and undismayed. When they turned back, she felt
stronger.

But Teb and Camery were standing beside an out-
cropping of boulders, arguing in harsh whispers, and
Teb's fury frightened Kiri anew.

20

WHAT HORRORS WILL QUAZELZEG BRING INTO TIR-
ROR? HIS POWER GROWS WITH EACH COUNTRY HE CON-
QUERS, WITH EACH PERSON HE ENSLAVES. AND AS IT
GROWS, IT MOVES CLOSER TO MY KING AND MY CHIL-
DREN.

Teb faced Camery angrily. "We could destroy Sivich
now! His troops are waiting below the cliff like sheep
for slaughter. If we fire-dive the camp, stampede the
horses, we can kill every man. What are you waiting
for?"

"If we attack here," Camery said, "Sivich and his
captains will escape into the caves. We don't know
those caves and tunnels; this mountain is honeycombed
with them." She shook her head. "We'd kill only their
soldiers, not the leaders. We'd kill *all* their soldiers,
even those who could be saved." She studied Teb,
puzzled by his anger. "Once they're out in the valley,

we can surround them. We can begin the battle with dragon song—with visions that will free so many—to fight for *us*."

Teb only looked at her coldly.

"We must free those soldiers who can be freed. We must give them a chance to turn on their masters." She touched his cheek, seeking for warmth in his face, and saw only rage. When he turned away, she stared after him, perplexed and afraid. What was wrong with him? She saw Kiri in the shadows and went to her.

"What's wrong? What happened in Aquervell?"

"Let me show you."

The visions were powerful. When Kiri was finished, Camery was filled with Teb's sickness. She watched his dark silhouette pacing the cliff and touched his thoughts—and recoiled.

"What shall I do?" she said sadly.

"Do just as you planned," Kiri said. "Attack Sivich. Surely in battle Teb will come right. There . . . there's nothing else we can do."

Camery nodded, and pushed back her pale hair. "Come on. Colewolf and Marshy are doctoring Ice-flower. I'll feel better when I'm doing something—I can think better." She took Kiri's hand, and they went up over the moonlit rocks. Perhaps they both needed Colewolf's steady comforting.

He was brewing herbs to press against Iceflower's wounds. Beside him, Marshy folded blankets for poultices. Iceflower lay quietly while Elmmira licked her torn flesh, cleaning it before the packs were laid on. The great cat reared against the young dragon and climbed over her with heavy, gentle paws. When Kiri and Camery began to soak the blankets and fold them over her wounds, Iceflower looked around at them with pleasure. "Warm," she said. "So warm." But then her eyes flashed with suspicion. "These wounds are only of the surface. You are not going to keep me from the battle? I am quite well enough to battle the dark armies. I am strong enough to kill a thousand dark soldiers."

Camery laughed and rubbed Iceflower's nose. "I expect you are. But you will be high above the clouds with your brothers and sister."

"Why? What use would we be up there?"

"That is the way it will be," Camery said. "You are our second line. You are to come down only if you are badly needed."

"But Rockdrumlin has already gone to battle," Iceflower argued.

"Rockdrumlin carries Charkky and Mikk against Auric Palace. I want the rest of you just where I said. You are very important—you will be there if we need you."

Iceflower looked at Camery steadily. Camery stared back. At last Iceflower subsided, calmed herself, and gave over to the warmth of the poultices. She had laid her head down, her eyes half closed, when a little cough made them turn.

A white fox stood in the moonlight, a broad grin on

his narrow white face, a look of rollicking high spirits. Kiri stifled a shout and grabbed him up in a hug, though she knew it destroyed his dignity.

"Oh, Hexet! It's so good to see you!"

"Hexet the Thief," Elmmira said, purring, stroking the fox with a big paw.

Hexet leaped down from Kiri's arms and began to groom himself, embarrassed at having been held. "The foxes of Nison-Serth are with me," he said. "They are trying to cheer Tebriel—or at least get him to be civil."

Kiri said, "He hasn't had an easy time."

"Seastrider told us. Pixen is trying to talk to him."

But when they looked, Teb had walked away from Pixen and all the foxes, was striding away alone, along the ledge. The foxes stood staring after him, dejected, their tails low.

Teb paced the cliff, angry and hurting and ashamed. He had never been rude to foxes. The foxes had saved him from capture in the caves of Nison-Serth, he had hidden in their dens and learned their secret ways, and he loved them well. Yet just now he had snapped at them and turned away. A deep hopelessness filled him, as if he could do nothing right—a driving hunger for defeat that made him feel even guiltier.

He stood staring morosely down the mountain, torn with anger and defeat, filled with pain at the little foxes' hurt.

He knew he had to change the way he was thinking.

He had to gather himself to fight. Despite his twisted thoughts, he burned to kill Sivich. Yet even his rage against Sivich, and his desire to win back Auric, seemed somehow useless.

The waiting for Sivich to move made him even more irritable. The man had to move out soon if he meant to attack Nightpool under darkness. Doubts and dark voices pulled at Teb. He paced the cliff, shunning the others, until well past midnight.

The rushing sound of an owl messenger winging to them stirred him. A big barn owl dropped down out of the wind, straight for Camery.

"He's saddling up," the masked owl whispered, "saddling up—moving out. . . ."

Word sped among the troops. Below the cliff they could hear the hushing of hooves as Sivich's mounted troops headed their horses toward the open plain. The rebel troops followed, working their way down the dark cliff.

When Seastrider nudged him, Teb swung to her back, slipped, then righted himself and swung up. He felt Kiri and Camery watching him. He sat on Seastrider scowling as the dragons rose on silent wings into the moonlit sky. They made straight up, to lift above the blowing clouds, out of sight.

Sivich had moved well away from the mountain, and the rebel troops were still hidden within the mountain's shadow, when the dragons dropped low and began to sing.

Dragon song shattered the night. Its images moved across the plain, filling the minds of Sivich's troops as water will fill empty bowls. A phantom sun spun to life, to brighten the valley. And the valley was peopled with riders from long-past generations. Sivich's soldiers stopped their horses, stared around them, and cried out as daylight flamed across the plain and the images of men and women and children traveled past them, laughing and calling to one another. They watched as the phantom travelers made camp.

They saw herders ringing bells that brought their sheep and goats galloping to cluster around them. They saw children harvesting wild grains with magical knives that cut the wheat by themselves. They saw a trading market, and so real was the vision that Sivich's soldiers dismounted and wandered among stalls of bright wares. They examined silk gowns that held the enchantments of love, tunics that would turn away any weapon, clay jugs of wine that would never grow empty. They stared into laughing, happy faces filled with a well-being that they had never felt.

Sivich's soldiers watched water wizards make springs bubble up from dry ground; they saw a woman who wanted music hold up her hand so that the birds came flocking and singing.

Sivich's dark captains shouted and pulled the staring men to the ground and beat them, but the men paid little attention. They rose again, to move within the dragon vision. They saw, for the first time in their lives, folk with Tirror's magic still on them, folk who were free and were their own masters. In the bright visions spun by dragons and bards, Sivich's dull soldiers saw a life they had never dreamed possible.

They had been cheated: The dark had taken their pasts and their freedom. They stared up at the dragons circling above them and understood what dragon song did—it gave them back themselves.

They knew, for the first time, that they need not follow the slave masters.

Not all the soldiers woke from their enslavement. Some were too far gone in the dark power. Those who did wake drew their swords and spurred their mounts and rode down their dark masters. Camery's troops, and the dragons, came storming to fight beside them. The awakened rebels slaughtered dark soldiers. Owls dove into the faces of terrified horses to stampede them. Great cats and wolves leaped for screaming riders. On the outskirts of battle, otters and foxes waited for those who escaped on foot. But in the confusion, five dark leaders spun their horses and sped away south, Sivich among them. Only Camery saw. . . .

Sivich, she shouted. *Sivich escapes.* She swung her sword wide as Nightraider came down over two escaping captains. She cut one from the saddle as Colewold slew the other. Ahead of them, Sivich fled.

He's mine! Teb shouted. Seastrider dove for Sivich's broad, humped shoulders. All confusion left Teb, his mind was clear and intent. With one hard thrust, his sword ran Sivich through. He pulled Sivich across his lap and stared down with triumph.

"I am Tebriel of Auric! Do you remember me?"

Sivich stared, his eyes bulging.

"You murdered my father. You kept me as slave. Do you remember me now? You murdered the King of Auric. Now *I* am King of Auric! *Do . . . you . . . remember . . . me?*"

Sivich gasped for breath, his lips white.

Get on with it. Seastrider said. *Finish him.*

Why should I hurry? I'm enjoying this.

That is just the point, Tebriel. Too much pleasure in the killing.

He killed my father. He took cold pleasure in that. Mind your own business.

This is my business. You don't need to enjoy killing so much.

Teb ignored her and watched with cold satisfaction as Sivich struggled. "Look on my face, killer of my father. His death was painful, and so will yours be. Perhaps you enjoy the kiss of the shark—for it is the sharks of the sea that will have you."

Seastrider swept out past the surf, and Teb dumped Sivich into the sea far from shore. They saw the big sharks gather. "All right," Teb said. "They'll finish him—get moving."

But Seastrider didn't race for the fighting; she slowed, slipping on the wind, turning to look back at him. "What is it, Tebriel? Something terrible pulls at you."

His thoughts stumbled in shadow.

"What's the matter with you, Tebriel?"

"Nothing's the matter." Why had they come here to threaten Sivich's troops? He shook his head, dizzy and angry, and blocked his thoughts from her. In the black spaces of his mind, something compelling spoke. Seastrider stared back at him, shocked, pressing her mind stubbornly into his.

"Stop it, Seastrider! You have no right."

"I have every right!" She glared at him, then suddenly she slapped her wings into the wind and joined the battle, slashing and belching flame. He could only cling, furious, refusing to touch his sword. She swept over Ebis's troops fighting Sivich's soldiers herself, though Teb refused to fight. He heard Ebis's shouting and he wanted . . . wanted . . . .

He woke out of blackness, to pull himself back from shocking thoughts that cut searing across his soul, sickening him.

He felt Seastrider's relief.

Dawn was coming. He saw Windcaller dive, banking close to him. Kiri raised her sword in salute. "You killed him! You killed Sivich!"

He nodded and raised his sword to her, and laughed. But his mind dropped again into confusion, and, unable to help himself, he reached out to the distant thoughts that spoke so softly—when he saw high in cloud a lone dragonling, he was infuriated that Rockdrumlin's triumphant voice cut across his own searching thoughts.

The palace is secure, Rockdrumlin shouted. *The rebels have taken it! Charkky and Mikk are in the tower, directing everything.*

Teb scowled with annoyance at Rockdrumlin's jauntiness and returned to the urgent voice that pressed so close. He ignored Seastrider's anger. When he looked into the northern sky, he knew the presence was near. He knew—he must call it, bring it now. . . .

No, Tebriel! No!

His mind reached out to the living black cloud that appeared over the mountains. He smiled as he watched it lift, shifting and swelling until it swept over the last ridges toward him.

21

SOMETIMES I DREAM THAT I CAN SPEAK BETWEEN
WORLDS, THAT I CAN CREATE A VISION THAT WOULD
TOUCH TIRROR EVEN AFTER I'VE GONE THROUGH THE
DOORS. BUT SURELY THAT IS ONLY A DREAM, A WISH
TO BE CLOSE TO THOSE I LOVE.

The black cloud dove at the battlefield, filling the
wind with its stink, and a thousand black wings beat
at the faces of dragons and bards, blinding them. Five
hundred wrinkled bat faces searched, red mouths
screaming; claws and teeth tore at living flesh as little
red eyes sought for tender throats.

Your throat—cover your throat, a bard shouted. *They
want blood.* Whose voice? Colewolf's? A voice that tore
Teb from confusion and slapped him back into truth—
to the horror that was swamping them, the horror of
his own treachery.

I did this, *I* led them here. . . .

No!

He swung his blade at the stinking black creatures, mad with shame and fury.

Across the battlefield, the creatures blinded Windcaller and forced her down, nearly smothering Kiri. Camery held her leather tunic tight around her throat as sharp claws tore at it. Beyond her, Colewolf fought the clinging bats with his knife. Small teeth found his throat. He stabbed the creature and jerked it away. A thousand wings battered, five hundred mouths tried to suck.

Blood ran down Camery's neck as Nightraider floundered on the wind—then Teb's thought exploded in her mind, pulling her back. *The lyre! Use the lyre! By the Graven Light, use it now....* The vamvipers downed their victims, then left them for others. Human throats were quickly wrapped in leather, but the animals had no protection. *The lyre, Camery! Use the lyre!*

Camery clutched at the harness, dizzy, as Nightraider plunged on the wind. The blackness of his thrashing wings and of hovering vamvipers smeared into one blackness. She pulled the sucking bats from Nightraider's wings, and from her own face, but there were so many. She felt so dizzy, terrified for her dragon, and terrified for herself.

"The lyre! Use the lyre!" Teb's voice cried, so far away. She pawed at the lyre, but its chain pulled across her, and the little lyre dangled dangerously on the wind. She jerked it back, cold with panic.

Suddenly Seastrider was above her.

The white dragon hovered beside Nightraider in a tangle of wings. Teb reached out for the lyre. Camery tried to swing it free and nearly fell. A cloud of vamvipers hit them. Nightraider twisted under their pummeling force and dropped, crashing through trees.

High above, the dragonlings bellowed with fury at the black cloud of vamvipers that broke apart in dizzying sweeps below them. They heard Teb shout, *The lyre! Use the lyre!*" and they wondered where Camery was. The vamvipers wheeled and dove below them, in killing waves.

"Dive on them!" Bluepiper roared. "Dive!"

"Burn them!" Firemont screamed. "Dive!"

"Wait," Marshy shouted. Something yellow was flapping and darting above the black cloud, screaming with a commanding voice that cut and stabbed. . . .

"A queen!" he yelled. "They have a queen!"

"Kill her!" screamed Iceflower.

The dragonlings dove, but the queen slipped between them and was gone. They separated and dove again. She dodged and fled. Below them the battlefield was a melee of falling horses and riders. The darting vamviper queen shivered as the dragonlings came at her again. When they had the queen trapped between them, she sped straight for Aven's throat. Bluepiper twisted and bit at her, but the yellow vamviper darted beneath him, out of sight.

Suddenly Aven dove into space.

He grabbed the queen, dropping through wind. He

clutched the squirming, leathery bat queen, amazed that he had actually caught her. When he squeezed her throat, she twisted and fought. Falling on the wind, he choked the vamviper queen until her bloody mouth gaped and she went limp. He was falling, falling. . . .

Bluepiper rose beneath him, a mountain of dragon. Aven sprawled onto Bluepiper's back, Bluepiper's sheltering wings blocking out the terror of empty space. Aven was still squeezing the vamviper queen. Below them, five hundred vamvipers faltered and wheeled, screaming at the death of their queen.

By the time Teb reached Nightraider, Camery lay unconscious across the black dragon's neck, her face and hands a mass of blood, the lyre beneath her shoulder. Teb pulled the lyre free. When he sounded the first silver note, the vamvipers exploded away from him. He brought out the lyre's voice with all the power he knew—and all across the battlefield the vamvipers swept up away, hissing. The remaining dark soldiers turned their shivering horses and fled. High up, the black cloud of vamvipers waited, faltering and shifting, confused by the loss of their queen. But as they swung in a black wave across the wind, a vision touched them and spoke to them.

On the battlefield, a Door had appeared, opening into darkness.

A woman stood within, beside a white dragon, a woman who seemed covered with light, her gown and tawny hair shining and the golden sphere at her throat burning like fire.

She was beckoning. Teb tried to cry out to her but could only swallow. She was beckoning to the black cloud above him. It trembled and shifted as the leaderless, panicked vamvipers darted and flew at one another.

Come through, she cried.

In Teb's hands, the lyre's song formed into words: *Go through. Go through the Door. . . .*

The vamvipers swept back and forth, stirring a stinking wind.

Go through, the lyre cried. *Go back to your own world. Go through the Door. Go back. . . .*

But the shifting cloud fled away toward the mountain and hovered above it like restless black smoke.

Meriden cried, *Come through! Come through the Door! Come through to me!*

The vamvipers returned, fluttering and tumbling across the wind.

Come through. . . .

The cloud shivered and paused. Then the Door sucked them through into blackness, as if sucking up blowing soot.

Time hung still in white emptiness.

When it began again, Meriden was gone. The Door was gone.

22

I FEAR THE CASTLE OF DOORS, YET I AM DRAWN TO
IT. PERHAPS IT IS THOSE VERY CONFLICTS WITHIN US
THAT MARK THE TRUE MYSTERY OF OUR HUMANITY.

———————⟶∞⟵———————

Teb stood unmoving, seeing nothing but the after-
vision of Meriden framed within the black Door. He
held Camery close when she clutched at him, white
and bleeding and shaken. In both their minds, the
vision of their mother burned.

She was alive. They had seen her. She had pulled
the vamvipers through. They had heard her voice,
stirring a painful childhood longing in them both.

All around them, the battlefield began to come to
life. Soldiers rose, horses staggered up. Folk who had
stood frozen by the vision began to assess their hurts
and to kneel over the sprawling wounded.

Camery touched the lyre. "Do the vamvipers swarm
around her now? In that other world? How can she
battle them?"

They looked at each other, stricken. "Don't think that," Teb said. "She has great power. Perhaps she has trapped them somewhere, away from her."

"She can't always have had such power. She would have used it to come home. Or to drive Quazelzeg out."

"This time, the power of the lyre was with her." He touched the lyre's strings.

It was silent, drained of its magic.

"Come," she said. "The dragons need us."

The two dragons were very quiet, waiting patiently for their bards, their poor faces streaked with blood. Camery put her arms up to Nightraider and held his great head to her. Both dragons' eyelids were slashed and bleeding so they could hardly see. She began to sponge Nightraider's lids with water from her flask as Teb examined Seastrider's eyes.

The dragons' eyes seemed undamaged. Their rough-scaled lids had served them well. Teb and Camery cleaned the blood away and stopped the bleeding by applying pressure with damp cloths. It was not long before both dragons felt better, tossing their heads and sweeping into the sky again, filled with fierce relief.

"They were frightened," Camery said.

"Yes. They're all right now. Let me see your throat." He pulled her leather collar away and mopped the blood off her neck.

The blood was from slashes along her jaw, barely missing the arteries. As he sponged her wounds, he was filled with a private, and terrible, thought.

Did Meriden know that he had led the vamvipers here? He had failed her dismally—he had failed them all. Thakkur's words burned in his thoughts. *Do not underestimate Quazelzeg and what he is capable of. Do not let your pride lead you.* . . .

But he had. He had done that and more. He had challenged Quazelzeg too soon, before he was ready. His weakness and impatience had almost killed them all.

He did not belong with the bards. He did not belong with dragons. As he watched the dragonlings descend out of the morning sky, he was filled with self-loathing and wanted only to be alone.

He had led the vamvipers to them in an act of sedition as evil as any the pawns of the dark could have accomplished. And, he thought with alarm, he *was* the dark's pawn now.

The dragonlings landed in a storm of wings. Marshy and Aven and Darba slid down and grabbed each other in a terrified, shaken hug.

"You did it," Darba screamed, shaking Aven. "You killed the queen!"

"You were wonderful," Marshy cried.

"I was scared," said Aven. They hugged the dragonlings and looked at Teb, waiting for a word of praise.

But Teb had turned away, too sick in spirit to praise anyone. He walked away by himself across the gory battlefield. Seastrider followed him, her eyes blazing with anger.

"Stop it, Tebriel. You are wallowing in self-pity!"

"I am a traitor. I nearly got everyone killed. I could have lost all Tirror. I am not a fit bard."

"That is stupid! You are not responsible for all of Tirror. You take too much on yourself—you wallow in vanity as well as self-pity!"

He stared at her, shocked and hurt.

"The vamvipers would have found us anyway—regardless of you! Don't you think Quazelzeg could guess that we would attack Sivich?"

"It would have taken them longer. The battle would have been finished."

"You don't know that. You are awash in senseless remorse. You will do more harm by that than by bringing any kind of evil here. Turn around, Tebriel, and look. Everyone is watching us. Do you mean to make a complete fool of yourself?"

Teb turned. The bards stood looking at him. Behind them the dragons stared. He saw Thakkur, standing on a rise, alone, watching him. Suddenly furious, he turned and went back to the bards and stood defiantly waiting for their censure.

We know your pain, Colewolf said. *How can we help but know it? Don't you think, Tebriel, that you do terrible harm by turning away from us? Don't you think you insult us? We need each other—we need you very much.*

"You cannot simply stop being a bard," Camery said. "You cannot simply stop bearing that responsibility because of Quazelzeg's poisons." Her green eyes blazed as fiercely as Seastrider's. "Any of us would have done the same, filled with his tortures and his drugs." She stepped close to him and touched his cheek. "But, Teb, neither can you take on more than your share."

We are with you, Colewolf said, *not against you.*

"Together," Kiri said, "we can drive out the evil." She took his hand, looking at him deeply. "We freed the children, Teb. We have two new bards—and it was at great cost to you. We will never abandon you. Do not abandon us. Fight beside us, not against us!"

He wanted to shout, I can't fight. He felt so tired, drained, with nothing left inside but shame and anger.

Yet as he stood there, he was sustained by Kiri's strength—by Camery's strength, by the strength of all of them. Kiri clung to him, wiping her fist across her eyes. In a little while she said, "Come, there are stretchers to be made, wounds to bind." She knelt by her pack, to find bandages. When Teb looked up, he saw Thakkur, still on a knoll, still watching him. Teb wanted to go to him but was too ashamed.

All over the valley animals and men were assessing their wounds and trying to help themselves, or to help others. Hexet woke to lick his wounds, then nudge at other foxes. Three wolves struggled up. Five others lay dead. Elmmira made her way slowly to Teb and Kiri. They examined the vamviper bites deep in her shoulder, and Kiri unstrapped her flask to wash them.

Mitta and Hanni came across the body-strewn

182

meadow, carrying packs filled with bandages and salves. They stopped to touch and whisper, to examine wounds and clean and bandage them. All around them soldiers and animals crouched over the fallen, calling their names, weeping for the dead. Small owls began to appear from the mountain. The big owls, Red Unat among them, had taken their toll of vamvipers, but they were wounded, too. Hanni brought salves to the bards and a flask of Mitta's soothing draft. Everyone kept glancing toward the mountains, half expecting another attack. Soon Camery sent the three bard children and the dragonlings winging up, to scan the mountains and coasts. Still Thakkur watched Teb. At last, Teb went to him.

"You find me a failure," Teb said. "I have failed. I did not heed your advice. I underestimated Quazelzeg, and he—"

Thakkur interrupted, holding up one white paw. "I find you a hero for enduring such tortures."

Teb shook his head. "You told me about pride—about taking too much on myself. I walked into Quazelzeg's lair and—and . . ." He stared at Thakkur, stricken. "Am I one of them now?"

"That is melodramatic, Tebriel. You are a dragonbard. You are the King of Auric. Perhaps . . ."

Teb stared at him miserably. "Perhaps what?"

"Perhaps . . . you had better start acting like both."

Teb looked at Thakkur, his look filled with bitterness, then he turned away.

"Neither bard nor king allows himself anger beyond self-discipline, Tebriel. A leader tempers his anger— particularly anger at himself. He controls and uses it."

Teb turned to look back at Thakkur.

"I have absolute faith in you, Tebriel—in your goodness, in your ultimate good sense." Thakkur put out a paw.

Teb hesitated. Then he knelt and took Thakkur's paw. Their eyes held for a long moment, in which Teb remembered much.

23

WE *MUST* CONFRONT THE DARK INVADERS. WE MUST CHOOSE THE HORRORS OF WAR, OR WE WILL LOSE THE FREEDOM TO CHOOSE. PERHAPS TOO MANY OF US HAVE ALREADY LOST THAT FREEDOM.

From across the battlefield, the rebel leaders began to gather. Ebis the Black came galloping up surrounded by his officers, sporting a bandage around his forehead and another on his arm. His black beard was matted with blood, and there were wounds across his face. He shouted to see the bards alive, leaped from the saddle, and hugged them nearly hard enough to break bones.

"Cursed, blood-sucking bats. We lost twenty men." He glanced toward the ridge as if he expected another attack.

"Camery has sent a patrol," Teb said.

"Very good," Ebis said, giving Camery a look of

approval. He joined the soldiers and otters in improvising stretchers. "I can take the worst wounded to Ratnisbon Palace," he said, "those who can be carried that far. My folk will care for them skillfully."

While Ebis's soldiers dug out a huge common grave for the human soldiers, the bards buried the animals with solemn ceremony. They marked their grave with stones laid in a circle to signify the endless sphere of life. The bards and dragons wove a song for them, and the living animals bowed down and grieved.

The dragonlings and children returned to say there were no troops beyond the mountains, no ships on the sea, no disturbance around Nightpool. There was a moment of powerful feelings as they said farewell to Ebis and those who had fought beside them, then the bards mounted up, the dragons lifted fast, and they headed for Auric Palace.

They sped across a light wind, the dragons stretching in wide, free sweeps, filled with the joy of freedom and with the healing silence after the shouting and screams of war. The bards looked at each other between glinting wings. This was freedom, this weightless lifting on the wind. They winged through a mass of heavy cloud and broke out into sunlight above Auric's broad green meadows, skirted by the sea beyond. Rising from the meadows alone stood Auric palace, its slate roof reflecting the sun.

Smoke rose beyond the north wall; when they were close, they could see that troops were burning trash.

The palace gardens were dry and weedy, the orchard trees dead. They could see broken windows, and some of the roof slates were gone. But no neglect could mar the symmetry of the five wings built of pale stone, the angled courtyard wall, the wide expanses of windows, the twenty chimneys.

Of all the gardens, only their mother's private walled garden was alive and green. Fed by a sunken spring, it was a tangle of branches and vines. It looked as if no one had entered it in years.

Four years, Camery thought. Four years since they had seen their home—twice that since anyone had cared for the grounds or the palace.

A crowd had gathered on the meadow outside the open gates, their shouts and cheers filling the wind. The dragons glided to the meadow in a ceremony of sweeping wings, and the bards slid down into welcoming arms—all but Teb. He remained astride.

Go on, Tebriel, they wait for you, they wait for their king, Seastrider said, bowing her neck to stare at him.

He remained on her back, not speaking, watching Camery embraced and exclaimed over, watching Kiri and Colewolf and the children made welcome. Soon Camery disappeared inside, surrounded by old friends. But when Teb's friends looked up at him and saw his expression, they turned away.

Go on, Seastrider repeated angrily.

But it was a shout from the tower that got his attention. "Hah, Tebriel! Hah, Teb!" Charkky and Mikk hung out over the stone rail, waving crazily at him.

He looked up at them and couldn't help but laugh. He shook his depression off like a dirty cloak and waved to them and shouted. The crowd turned back to watch him, and when he slid down off Seastrider's back, he was surrounded at once, by friends he hadn't seen since he was a little boy. He was hugged and kissed and swept into the palace by the laughing crowd.

Inside, Camery was standing alone in the center of the great hall, looking. All the others had gone back to their tasks, giving her space and time for a private homecoming. She stood quite still, the sunlight from the windows touching her face. It was in that moment, watching her, that Teb knew how hard it had been for her to enter the palace again.

She had remembered her home as bright and filled with beauty, the rooms clean and sunny, their mother's rich tapestries covering the walls, the touch of their mother everywhere. She had come in, just now, wishing it could be like that, but expecting it to be filthy and decayed from the mistreatment of Sivich's soldiers.

It was neither filthy nor as they remembered from childhood.

The big, high-ceilinged hall was bare of furniture. It smelled of lye soap and plaster. Folk were hard at work everywhere, on ladders and on their hands and knees, scrubbing walls and floor and repairing holes in the white plaster and in the stone. Teb watched

Camery until she turned and put her hand out; then he went to her.

She said, "I can see Mama here. And Papa—when we were little, and so happy." They stood remembering the perfect time of childhood. But he soon grew cross and restless again—moody; he kept having such changeable moods. He seemed to have no control over them. But shame at his weakness only drew evil closer. He soon wandered away from Camery, with Quazelzeg's whispers close around him as he paced the empty corridors and abandoned rooms, driven by an impotent need for escape.

Kiri climbed one flight and another, looking into chambers, seeing the palace as it was now, but also as she had envisioned it from Teb's thoughts, the warm comfort it had once held. In two wings, the rooms had been swept clean, the windows washed. Beds stood without mattresses, and there wasn't much furniture left. Three wings hadn't yet been cleaned; the rooms were littered with garbage and bones. At the top of the third flight was a room that rose alone above all the rest. It was so sunny, so inviting, that she went in.

It smelled of soap, and the floor was still damp from scrubbing. There was no furniture. The room was five-sided. Each side had a deep bay of windows that looked down over one wing of the roof. A stone fireplace stood between two bays, laid with logs and kindling. The windows were open to let in fresh air and sunshine. A new mattress, still smelling of fresh straw, lay on the floor in one bay. This would be Tebriel's room—the room of the King of Auric.

"No, it will be kept for Meriden," Teb said behind her. She swung around, startled. She hadn't heard him come in or sensed him there.

"Meriden is still the queen," Teb said, coming to stand beside her. She took his hand. She could see a deep, irritable unrest in his eyes.

"She must have been happy here, Teb."

"I'm afraid for her. I keep seeing her standing in the blackness of those far worlds."

"Your mother is a brave warrior—a strong woman."

"For nine years she's been wandering among those worlds—among impossible terrors, impossible evil. Nine years, Kiri!"

"Maybe time is not the same there—not the same for her. And there must be good there, Teb, as well as evil. The light must have touched those worlds."

His dark eyes searched hers.

"She is strong, Teb. You must not lose hope for her. She was strong enough to pull the vamvipers through."

"What else does she plan? How can we help her? She—she will despise me, now, for calling the vamvipers to us."

"Any of us could have—"

"Save me that. I'm tired of being told that anyone could have turned traitor. I'm the one who nearly killed us all. Not one among you would have done what I did."

Kiri moved away and stood with her back to the stone wall, watching him. This was not the Tebriel she knew. She looked and looked at him, and he looked back, remorseful and defiant.

"You can't do this to yourself," she said softly. "You are caught in Quazelzeg's thoughts—not your own thoughts."

"That doesn't make sense. Try to make sense, Kiri."

"You are wallowing in self-pity!"

His eyes blazed with anger.

"Self-pity!" she shouted, losing control. "You are filled with it!"

"What do *you* know about self-pity? What do *you* know about being drugged and beaten? What do you—"

"*That's* self-pity! You are speaking Quazelzeg's words!"

They stood facing each other, furious and hurting.

"Listen to me," Kiri said evenly. "Maybe . . . maybe something positive has come from this."

He started to speak, but she stopped him. "Just listen. If the vamvipers hadn't found us, you would not have seen your mother. You wouldn't know she's alive."

"That's—"

"Listen! It took a terrible threat for your mother to reach out to you—for her to summon the *power* to reach out. Maybe . . . maybe the effort she made helped her. Maybe it increased the power she can command."

He stared at her, a spark of hope touching him. Then he shook his head and turned away. She went to him and touched his cheek. He looked so uncertain and lonely, locked in his private darkness. She tried to keep her voice soft, to keep the anger out of it. "Quazelzeg *wants* to make you doubt, Teb. He *wants* to make you hate and turn away from us."

He looked deeply at her, his eyes filled with resentment and anger—but with need for her. She put her arms around him, and suddenly he drew her close. Suddenly he let himself hold her tight, burying his face against her hair. They stood for a long time in the warm sunlight, saying nothing.

When the sun moved and put them in shadow, he stirred and held her away to look at her. "Maybe . . . maybe you're right. Maybe I should listen more to where my anger comes from."

"Just . . . just don't turn away from us."

"I want . . . suddenly I want to go down to Mama's garden. It's . . . where I remember her best."

He led her out of the bright room and down a back way and out to a high wall. The gate in it was stuck or locked. He climbed it finally by the crossbars and opened it from inside.

It was the tangled, wild garden she had seen from the sky. Rosebushes and one giant flame tree grew up the walls, so thick she could hardly see the bricks.

There were small fruit trees let run wild, smothered in grass and flowers. A stone bench before the flame tree was grown over with low branches of its red blooms. Teb pushed them away and drew her down beside him.

He showed her Meriden sitting on the stone bench with the two small children—himself and Camery. The vision of Teb was fuzzy, a feeling more than a figure. He showed Meriden tucking him into bed, singing a strange little song to him, showed her holding court with their father, surrounded by officials. He made a vision of a family supper alone in the high chamber, and of court suppers in the great hall. He showed Meriden galloping her mare across the meadows playing tag with the children, laughing when their ponies caught her. Kiri felt undone by the visions, so private and warm, and important to him. Scenes tumbled one atop the other as the children grew older, until the morning they stood at the gate watching their mother ride away, not to return to them. When the last scene faded, Teb's arms were around her. She held him, shaken with the loss that seven-year-old Teb had felt.

He put her away from him at last, and took Meriden's diary from his pack. He leafed through it, and began to read to her from scattered passages. He read until the sun left the garden, and he had reached the last written page, with just one short entry at the top.

"This is the last entry I will make. I am in the sunken city, and I leave the diary here. I will go through the Door now, into other worlds—to find the dragon,

*and to seek the source of the dark, and perhaps learn
how to defeat it. I love you, my children. I love you,
my dear king."*

As they stared at each other, Kiri knew the supple
forming of his thoughts, felt feelings and images unfolding in a pattern that suddenly shocked her. Suddenly she knew the decision he had made—it struck
across her mind sharply. She looked at him, terrified.

"I *must* go, Kiri. I must search for her—I've known
that for a long time. She means to draw Quazelzeg to
her through the Doors; she calls him to her.
She . . . perhaps she cannot fight him alone."

"But you must not go there alone. I—"

"*No!* This I must do alone—not out of pride, believe
me. Only one bard must go there. You—the rest—
must remain . . . to battle Quazelzeg with all the
strength you have among you. To . . . to battle for me,
from this side."

They held each other, their minds joined, the urgency of his commitment filling them. But her fear for
him—and his own fear—blew like a dark curtain between them.

"Yes, I'm afraid," he said softly. "But it's time—to
face Quazelzeg. I must do this, Kiri."

When they drew apart, and he reached to close Meriden's diary, his face went white. A new entry shone
where, moments before, the page had been half blank.

It was in the same bold black stroke. It was Meriden's writing.

The Castle of Doors is carved into the mountains of Aquervell. Now that I have come through, I know better the nature of the Doors and of the Castle. Some of the rooms are caves; some are built of stone. But they are without number, and each room has a Door leading to a world, and the worlds, too, are without number.

A vision filled their minds of mountains thrusting up scoured by fitful winds, and ridges snaking away broken by caverns and man-made bastions. The scene shifted and changed, disappearing beyond fogs and coming close and sharp as time shifted. Only the center held steady, a stone vortex of angled roofs and towers growing from mountain ridges. The image held them, the power of the Castle of Doors held them.

"Maybe only there," Teb said, "lies the power to defeat Quazelzeg and the unliving." They bent over the page together and read silently.

I sense the increasing power of the dark. And I feel the power of the Graven Light. I know both powers grow stronger, confronting each other with relentless and steady intent. If I can draw Quazelzeg here, away from Tirror, I think I can destroy him. I must try. My powers are stronger now.

Take care, Tebriel. I know that you will come searching for me. I cannot prevent that. And I need you—but not before you are ready. Take care—that the dark within you does not triumph.

They sat stricken, touching the page. Meriden knew

too well what fevers swept his mind—knew, as Thakkur knew. Thakkur's warnings filled him, too. *Take care, Tebriel, when you journey into Sharden. You are not invulnerable. Do not do this alone.* Thakkur's voice was as clear as Meriden's, as if both were there with him, watching him.

Yet in this one thing, Teb knew, Thakkur was wrong. He must do this alone, no one else must go from Tirror. He looked at Kiri, torn between Thakkur's wisdom, the threat to Tirror, and his mother's need. Meriden must not face Quazelzeg alone. Perhaps she had done all she could to draw Quazelzeg away from Tirror, perhaps she needed him desperately now.

Certainly the other bards did not need him—with the dark, traitorous winds that swept him, he was the weakest among them.

This thought alone should have held him back, should have made him turn away from confronting Quazelzeg and endangering Meriden. But it did not. It only fired his determination to conquer that weakness—by facing the greatest challenge he could face. By defeating Quazelzeg and saving Meriden—by saving Tirror. Thakkur's whisper, *Do not let your pride lead you,* went unheeded.

Kiri, shaken with fear, moved into his arms and pressed her face against him. She held him tight, willing him to stay. He pulled away and cupped her face in his hands.

"I mean to go at once. Seastrider and I must go alone."

"You must not. That is what you must *not* do. That is exactly what Thakkur warned you about. Oh, please, you must not face the dark alone. Please, Teb. Face Quazelzeg within the love and strength of all of us together. We will all go together, battle him together. Not alone. Not—"

His flaring anger silenced her. "If you care for me, if you know me and care for me, you know I must do this alone." He reached to remove the lyre.

"No!" she shouted. "No! If you must go alone, then you must take the lyre!" Her fear and anger were terrible. "You will not go into Sharden without it!" She stood defying him until he dropped the lyre back against his tunic.

As he turned away, she stood looking after him filled with the one consolation, that the lyre would give him strength.

24

WITHIN QUAZELZEG'S EASTERN PALACE THERE IS A
DOOR MADE OF GOLD THAT CAN OPEN BY A WARPING
OF TIME AND PLACE INTO THE CASTLE OF DOORS—
JUST AS THE DOOR IN THE SUNKEN CITY DID. YET
ONLY IF OUR OWN POWER FALTERS DOES QUAZELZEG
HOLD CERTAIN CONTROL OVER HIS PRIVATE GOLD DOOR.

Teb and Seastrider left well before it was light. His
thoughts were filled with what lay ahead, but filled,
too, with Thakkur's dark eyes watching him. He had
so strong a sense of Thakkur that the white otter might
almost have been with him. His mind echoed Thakkur's
warnings of danger and foolish pride—and of the fool-
ishness of battling the dark alone. Thakkur's voice rode
with him for a long way, unsettling him, nearly making
him turn back. But then Thakkur's more positive words
came. *I have absolute faith in you, Tebriel—in your
goodness. . . .*

When thoughts of Thakkur faded, the wind rushed empty around Teb. Alone on the wind, bard and dragon remained silent, winging north toward Aquervell and the city of Sharden.

It took Kiri hours to go to sleep. She tossed on her straw pallet, trying not to wake Camery. Her fear for Teb was a blackness that would not leave her. She knew that when she woke in the morning, Teb and Seastrider would be gone—alone. When finally she did sleep, she dreamed a vision so real she thought she and Teb had returned to Nightpool.

She dreamed that Seastrider and Windcaller dropped onto the sea beside Nightpool, and all around them otters came hurrying out of caves, shouting and hah-hahing in greeting. She dreamed that she and Teb followed Thakkur and Hanni into the sacred cave amid a press of eager, fishy-smelling otters. There, Thakkur turned and looked at her with such powerful concern and said, "I can give you this, I can give Tebriel this, though it pains me."

She dreamed that the clamshell had brightened, and when the vision came, all who watched were caught in the black emptiness between worlds. She saw the ivory lyre lying alone, across ancient white bones. She saw Quazelzeg moving through dark worlds following a shadow she could not make out, and she screamed with fear for Teb. She awoke sweating and cold.

In his palace at Aquervell, Quazelzeg followed Meriden in vision, meaning to turn her back to Tirror, where his power over her would be greatest. She kept retreating, glancing back at him, laughing as she slipped in and out of shifting dimensions beside the white dragon. He did not like her mockery; he did not like the insolent turn of her head. She thought that she led him, that she had drawn him through again. But *this* was only a vision. He would follow her thus until she fled from him into evils she had not dreamed; then she would beg for his help.

A river lay ahead. Meriden and the dragon flew across it. Rivers contained creatures friendly to him, and he stepped in. When slimy hands reached, he smiled. This was, after all, only vision. But the creatures clutched at him. When he pushed them away, their mouths sucked at his hands and arms, burning like fire. He turned, puzzled—she had drawn him through against his will. He brought his power to drive the creatures back, to free himself. But Meriden and the dragon stood before him.

Behind them opened a Door into a cave, and in the cave shone the giant white skeleton of a dragon. Its tall ribs curved up in an arch, and its empty eye sockets held shadows that shifted and threatened him—as if Bayzun's spirit lived. Meriden smiled coldly.

"The spirit of Bayzun will defeat you," she said softly "The Ivory Lyre of Bayzun will defeat you."

Quazelzeg backed away, willed himself away from

her; with a terrible effort he willed himself back into his palace.

He stood there shaken.

This moment made an end to games. The woman must be disposed of. He shouted for Shevek. The captain came running.

"I expect to be in Sharden by tomorrow night. I do not relish a long ride. Find a fast ship."

Shevek nodded.

Quazelzeg smiled. In Sharden his powers would increase. In Sharden he could step *through* at his own choosing, by the power of the gold Door, and move on within the Castle of Doors readily, to find Meriden. Soon Tebriel would arrive in Sharden, and the spells Quazelzeg had planted within the bard—and the bard's own weakness—would feed his own power further.

Kiri woke to sunlight in her face. Camery's bed was empty. She lay seeing the dream. *Was* it a dream? Or, as she slept, had Thakkur given her a vision? Her thoughts were filled with the shadows of dark worlds and with Quazelzeg's pale, evil face; and with the shock of the ivory lyre lying abandoned across ancient bones. Waking fully, she remembered that Teb would be gone from Auric now, winging over far continents, and she buried her face in her pillow.

At last she rose, washed from the basin of cold water Camery had left, and dressed. She did not feel hungry. She went down the stone flights, thinking only of Teb.

The main hall was crowded with folk packing bundles, wrapping food, mending and oiling harness and boots. The courtyard was the same, as people prepared to journey north. Teb's desire to hurry northward had flamed through the palace, filling everyone with the need to follow him.

Camery came to join her.

"He wasn't ready," Kiri said. "He isn't ready to face Quazelzeg."

"No one is completely ready to do that, Kiri. But now, all of Tirror will follow him, to confront those on Aquervell." Camery's green eyes were filled with resolve. "It is time. Teb has made it so. And perhaps our mother has, too."

Within an hour, the bards and dragons were in the sky, lifting above banks of gray cloud. Below, the march north had begun, flowing out of Auric's palace and villages, and from the palace at Ratnisbon, gathering more strength as it moved north. Perhaps no one could put logic to this sudden swelling movement, but already it was inevitable and fierce. The dragonbards meant to free all who might join it.

Camery and Marshy moved to the west, bringing song and freedom to the outer islands. Colewolf and Aven followed to the east, touching the larger countries. Kiri and Darba and the two riderless dragonlings moved up through the center of the island mass. Below them the marching numbers swelled as the bards and dragons freed more and more of Tirror's peoples, waking slaves in a sudden all-out attack on the remaining pockets of darkness. Those slaves turned on their masters and killed them. Everywhere, they were joined by the speaking animals. Off the eastern coast, otters flashed through the green waters, led by the two white otters, moving resolutely and unswervingly north.

Thakkur forged on, grimly cleaving through the sea's swells. He had done all he could. His love was with Teb, his caring and his deep prayers. He felt certain that they approached the last battle, and he knew a dread he did not speak of, a private sadness.

25

AS SHARDEN FELL, FROM A CITY OF VIVID LIFE TO A
PRISON OF DESPAIR, SO ALL TIRROR NOW FOLLOWS.

———⚬———

Teb and Seastrider crossed over the last islands just
at dusk and made for the Aquervell shore, dropping
low over cadacus fields that grew along the coast. The
city of Sharden rose beyond the fields, a tangle of close,
narrow streets running at all angles and crowded with
shacks and stone mansions pushing against one another. The city was built along and over three rivers,
its seventeen bridges each crusted with houses and
shops divided by a narrow cobbled lane. On a hill apart
from Sharden stood Quazelzeg's castle, a fortress of
dark-gray stone.

Sharden had once been the jewel of Tirror. It was
the center where all craftsmen had come to study, to
trade, to celebrate and feast. The shops had been filled
with wares wrought half with skill and half with magic—

cloth of gold reflecting distant visions, kettles of copper that could brew an ambrosia of healing, bridles that could immediately gentle the wildest colt. That magic was gone now; the city was a morass of dirty streets and bawdy houses and drug dens and theaters where a night's entertainment watching unspeakable tortures could be had for the price of a new victim—a child or small animal.

Seastrider circled high above the clouds until nighttime. When they could not be seen, she dropped down to a rocky hill beyond palace and city, where she could lie hidden among jutting boulders. From here Teb could see the palace and the guards pacing atop its wall.

He ate a simple supper of dried meat and bread, wondering if he should slip into the palace when most of its inhabitants slept, to find the gold Door. Perhaps that would be the easiest way through into the Castle of Doors. There were two such Doors, far from the Castle of Doors but opening into it by spells. Meriden had gone through the other Door, in the sunken city, to move through warping space into the Castle of Doors and so into other worlds. If Meriden had been able to move through that Door, surely he and Seastrider could enter through this one.

The other way would be to fly north over the mountains until they saw the castle as they had seen it in Meriden's vision—but the gold Door was so near. Surely he could get to it unseen when the palace slept.

"And how would *I* get into the palace, Tebriel? How

would I squeeze myself into palace chambers, to reach the gold Door? No, Tebriel. Not possible. We must go over the mountains."

"Yes, all right," he said, keeping his own counsel. "But tonight we must rest. It was a long journey from Auric. You flew against heavy winds." Strangely, now that he was here, he was not ready. Something held him back. He wondered if Meriden's will held him . . . *not before you are ready. Take care. . . .*

Seastrider looked at him uneasily. Yet if he wanted sleep, so be it. She curled down between the boulders, to rest and keep watch. He lay down against her.

He could hear, from the city, the faint sounds of horses and wagons, doors slamming, and scattered shouts. When it grew late, the shouts increased, mixed with harsh music. The city drew him, with its tangle of narrow streets and of different peoples. He turned over, away from it, and at last he slept.

He woke to far, raucous laughter and the terrified screams of a child. He sat up and didn't sleep anymore.

Near to midnight, a coach arrived at the palace from the east, its six horses gleaming with sweat in the torchlight. Soldiers snapped to attention, and servants backed away in deference as a tall, hunched figure stepped out—a figure that struck terror into Teb.

As he watched Quazelzeg enter the palace, Teb's urgency to go through the Doors faltered again. By the time the palace quieted and lamps were snuffed, he had worked himself into a turmoil of doubt.

Quite late, he began to see snatches of vision.

He saw Meriden. All around her swirled dimensions ever changing—meadow, wood, hellfire, stars, swamp, blackness. He saw a cave that was a dragon's tomb, the giant white skeleton looming, and, afraid, he turned away from it. He wandered through shifting worlds stumbling and confused.

But slowly the confusion left him. The hunger that Quazelzeg had planted through drugs and mind warping grew bold. He began to lust for the drugs, to need them, and to hunger for the powers the drugs would give him.

Those powers, he thought with sudden understanding, were powers he could use to drive the dark out, not to help it—if he was clever.

If he was canny, he could outsmart Quazelzeg. With the powers the drugs gave him—powers Quazelzeg had meant him to use for the dark—he could defeat the un-man. With those terrible powers he had touched when he lay in Quazelzeg's palace, he could control Tirror and control everyone in it. And then, instead of helping the unliving, he would force every soul upon Tirror to rise against the unliving and drive the dark out.

How simple. And how foolproof. He had only to make Quazelzeg think he had turned to the dark.

When he had such power, he would permit only goodness upon Tirror. Hadn't Thakkur himself said, *I have—faith in you, Tebriel—in your goodness, in your ultimate good sense.*

His need to control was different from Quazelzeg's

greed for control. He, Tebriel, wanted only to save Tirror. He needed the drugs to strengthen his powers—he would take of the powers of the unliving and join them with his own powers, and thus make himself invincible.

He *would* save Tirror.

He would find drugs easily in Sharden, on any street corner. He was completely caught in the brilliance of his plan, when suddenly Seastrider struck him across the face, knocking him backward. He stared at her, shocked.

"He steals your soul, Tebriel! He takes your soul from you!"

"He does nothing of the kind! What's the matter with you?"

"He is sending visions to destroy you! He is drawing your mind into the darkness!"

"His thoughts are not touching me! Leave me alone!"

Seastrider reared over him. Her power hit him like a storm; her eyes blazed as she sought to destroy Quazelzeg's hold. She breathed out fire and cuffed him, and drove him up the hill farther from the city and palace. He could not use a sword against her any more than he could thrust it through his own body. She cornered him among boulders. He fought her with his bard powers, defying her with a fury he had never imagined he would feel for her. But for every movement he made, she bested him. She would not let him leave the hill.

In the small hours, when he saw he could not win, he pretended to falter. He rolled into his blanket and made a skillful vision of sleep.

Seastrider did not sleep. Each time he glanced up, she was watching him.

Across the continents the pilgrimage was now a strong army marching steadily north. Slaves had become soldiers. The cats and wolves and otters and foxes hunted food for the humans and shared the children's beds to warm them. No one was turned away; all had a right to confront the dark on Aquervell.

But the unliving, too, marched north.

Quazelzeg was not yet ready for Teb to enter the Castle of Doors. Deftly he wove visions for Tebriel through the power he held over him, renewing the black chambers of confusion that he had erected in Tebriel's mind and renewing the bard's drug hunger.

The twisted visions sucked at Teb in grand vistas of power, so he hardly remembered that he and the bards together—or even he and Meriden—might already possess the power to draw the unliving away from Tirror and destroy them. He clung to the grander plan. He fought his confusion sometimes, sweating and trapped in the consuming pit of Quazelzeg's will. But more often he followed the dark dream. Day came, then night again. He made no move to set out for the mountains. Seastrider did not sleep but watched him steadily. She would not allow him to leave the hill. When dark soldiers skirted the base of the hill, Seastrider drove them off, raging at Teb to fight them.

Teb would not. He turned away from her, nursing his own thoughts. For two days he dreamed his grand dream and longed for the power-strengthening drugs, and waited for Seastrider to sleep. He did nothing to help Meriden.

Late on the second night, when Seastrider could no longer keep awake, when she dozed in spite of a terrible effort of will, Teb moved away from her down the dark, rocky hill. The craving drew him powerfully. If, in some dark recess of his mind, it terrified him, too, he ignored that. The black desire pulled him on, toward the night sounds of Sharden.

Sharden's streets were narrow, rubbish-strewn, and dim. He stumbled through them eagerly. The city smelled of stale food and animal dung . . . and drugs. Ahead of him, shouting crowds had gathered for some brutal entertainment. Teb hurried to them, drawn by the scent of cadacus.

He found cadacus easily, all he wanted, and licked it from dirty spoons like any drug-ridden creature. Folk watched him, interested. When he was well drugged, they moved in and began to shove and caress him. But when two men ripped his tunic open, he clutched the exposed lyre, shocked into sense—and terror. His tormentors paused, staring at the lyre. Drug-crazy men and women surrounded him, reaching for it.

He backed away from them, protecting the lyre drunkenly. The horde pressed close. He struck the lyre's strings into harsh music to drive them back. Its power stopped them; they stood shivering and gaping.

But when he turned away, they followed. He fled, reeling, through narrow rubbled streets, using the lyre's music to drive them back. But as he ran, the lyre suddenly fell silent. The dark hordes gained on him. Thakkur's warning rang in his head—and a sudden, sick dismay overcame him.

It was thus Seastrider found him, pursued by a lusting rabble through alleys. She dove, tearing down walls to get at him, breaking buildings and driving men back against shattered timbers and into distant streets. He stood watching her sweep toward him and was filled with love for her—and with shame.

She dragged him up into the sky, carried him back to the hill, and dropped him on his blanket. She stood staring down at him, her long green eyes cold with disgust.

"What is your excuse tonight, Tebriel? You were not chained to a table tonight. You were not force-fed cadacus tonight.

"This night's stupidity was your own doing! Tonight, you used the magical powers of the lyre, which were meant to save our world—*you used them to save yourself!* To save your own hide from the terrible results of your stupid, blundering weakness!"

He stared up at her, flayed raw by her fury. She didn't need to be so violent when he felt this sick.

"Why have you come here to Aquervell? Do you remember that, Tebriel?"

"What makes you so angry?"

"You do. Your stupidity does. Your weakness makes me retch with disgust."

He wanted to slap her. "What do you mean to do about it?"

"It is not what *I* will do about it. It is what you will do. What *do* you mean to do, Tebriel?"

He looked at her coldly. But he realized, with sick shame, that only Seastrider's anger kept him from sinking completely under Quazelzeg's power. When she changed suddenly from anger, and her eyes became dark with hurt, he stared at her, shaken. Her voice became softer and incredibly sad.

"Do you know, Tebriel, how difficult it is for me to rage at you thus? Do you know how it tears at me? I want to comfort you. I want only to curl around you and warm and comfort you."

He stared at her uneasily—this wasn't fair.

"The drug hunger possesses you, and I cannot fight it. Kindness cannot fight it. Kindness can only weaken you."

He started to speak, but her look stopped him.

"Only you can fight this, Tebriel. Only you can defeat it. I cannot." Her look was the saddest he had ever seen. "If you do not fight it—and win—you will destroy us both. And you will destroy Meriden."

He felt shame so sharp he could not look at her.

He knew what he must do—now, before he could falter again. He trembled with terror of Quazelzeg and of the dark worlds, and of how the dark might reach him beyond that barrier. But Meriden struggled alone to draw the dark away from Tirror and to stop a larger invasion. He must go there at once, to help her, before his courage failed altogether.

It did not occur to him to wonder why, when Quazelzeg could mold his mind so readily, he still felt driven to go into those distant worlds to help Meriden. Whatever occurred to Seastrider she kept to herself. Perhaps her wisdom told her that not until the challenge was faced could he be free.

As dawn began to lighten the sky, Teb made ready in a dull silence born of drug sickness. Seastrider was quiet. But once he was mounted, she leaped powerfully into the slate-gray sky, pulled fast above the concealing clouds, and swept north.

26

WITHIN THE DOORS, TIME AND DISTANCE ARE AS NOTH-
ING. ONE CAN BE AS CLOSE AS A BREATH AND AS FAR
AWAY AS FOREVER. I PRAY TO THE GRAVEN LIGHT TO
HELP US. I THINK IT IS THE ONLY POWER THAT CAN.

Quazelzeg's chambers in the palace at Sharden were
crusted with jewels stolen from a thousand worlds, his
furniture covered with gold leaf and inlaid with plat-
inum, his carpets woven of rare silks and human hair.
In the small hours before dawn, he stood among the
rich furnishings locked in vision.

He watched Tebriel and his dragon wing north toward the Castle of Doors, and he smiled. The bard
had fought a ridiculously heroic battle within himself—
and was caught as surely as a fox is caught in a trap.

Young Tebriel wanted to help his mother. How very
touching. Oh, yes, the link between mother and son
was strong. But Tebriel's midnight journey into Shar-

den and his obedience to the dark powers had weakened both of them. Afterward, it had been easy to drive Meriden back when she appeared to him again. She had retreated quickly. Yes, young Tebriel had strengthened the dark's powers considerably.

Quazelzeg was satisfied that now Meriden no longer had the power to pull *him* through into other worlds. Now he would enter only as he chose. Very soon, she would no longer hold any barrier against the hordes he would call into Tirror.

It was not easy to bring the dark creatures through; it had not been easy to bring the vamvipers. It took great concentration to master them and draw them from endless worlds. With Meriden and her interference, it was even more difficult.

But she would not hold them back much longer. Through Tebriel, a rent had been torn in the power she had laid down. Soon a wraith or incubus would slip through, and her power would be further weakened. One barrier down, and the dark creatures would break all barriers and swarm into the city. Then Tirror would be his completely. Not even the lyre could fight such an army.

Meantime, managed skillfully, mother and son could be played against each other.

It was fortunate that last night Tebriel had used the lyre. Now it would take some time for the lyre to replenish its magic.

Meriden's words echoed unpleasantly. *The Ivory*

Lyre . . . will defeat you. The spirit of Bayzun will defeat you. . . .

But that would not happen now. The lyre was silent. And very soon the lyre would belong to him, would belong to the world of the dark.

Teb and Seastrider flew through a dawn as gray and desolate as winter. They recalled the vision of the Castle of Doors and scanned the deep mountain ravines and tall peaks, which became wilder as they moved north. But not until late afternoon did they see the familiar tangle of shifting domes and ridges crowded around the center. Seastrider dropped low to wing down shadowed chasms, seeking a way in.

They followed winding ravines and twisting ridges. Flying back and forth, they circled towers, searching, until they nearly lost hope of finding a way in. But suddenly, as they soared through a shaft of bright sun, Seastrider swerved through a black slit between mountains.

Blackness swallowed them; they spun, sucked down.

Valleys dropped below them miles deep, only to turn into peaks thrusting miles high. Caves and tunnels twisted into uncounted rooms that vanished, to be replaced by others. Seas became deserts; the sky darkened into night and suddenly burned with day again. Winds whipped at them and lifted and dropped them, and were gone. As the world around them shifted, Teb's nerve failed. How could they find Meriden here?

How could any invasion of dark creatures be discovered, and held back, in this nightmare?

As flotillas of boats pushed across the strait toward Sharden's city, the eight dragons, too, crossed the last stretch of sea. They passed over palace and city and dropped down among giant boulders on the rocky hill. They knew that Teb and Seastrider had been there on the hill and that they had gone. Kiri was cold with terror for Teb, close to panic, and held steady only by the strength of the others. They watched from among the boulders as the armies of light pulled their boats onto the shore and gathered across Sharden's hills. There were dark troops camped around the palace. The power of the dark reached out and kindled terror in the rebels and animals, but so powerful was the rebels' commitment that no one thought to turn back. Scattered campfires sprang up as folk made hasty meals.

Seastrider flew on through streaming light and through blackness, searching the stone twistings and echoing spaces. Neither she nor Teb knew how they would find Meriden, but they shouted her name. Their cries were swallowed by the vast spaces. Was there anything to hear them? Seastrider leaped chasms and sped down twisting tunnels between shifting walls that opened suddenly into emptiness or closed before them in barriers of stone.

As they fled through endless worlds, they knew that

the armies of light had attacked Quazelzeg's palace, flanked by the diving dragons. They saw the soldiers of the unliving crouched in masses along the palace wall. As time shifted, the cries of the battle echoed down otherworld chambers. Winter and summer met them and were lost; worlds fell away and other worlds loomed; and visions of the battle followed them.

How long they forged ahead, they couldn't guess. They knew only that Tirror was caught in a terrible and decisive war, and that still they had no clue how to stop it—how to drive back the dark, how to prevent more dark creatures from pouring through, how to find Meriden. Teb's mind was nearly drowned in confusion, when he began to hear Meriden's voice echoing down vast distances. . . .

Tebriel . . .

Seastrider swerved toward it.

Tebriel . . .

They swerved again and dove through tunneled chambers.

The grave, Tebriel—find the grave of Bayzun. Find the cave where Bayzun lies in death. . . .

They twisted and sped like hounds, following Meriden's echoing shout.

Bayzun's cave . . .

Suddenly Seastrider banked and slipped across the wind into a gigantic well of air circled by steep mountain walls.

The chasm was so deep they could not see the bottom, only mist. A far, small hole of sky shone above them. The well was washed by winds that lifted and played like churning waters. In the side of a mountain yawned a cave. Something white gleamed deep inside. Seastrider banked to it.

Inside the cave loomed the white skeleton of the great dragon, sire of all Tirror's dragons. The arch of his white ribs melted away into darkness, supporting the thick white spine, then letting it down to snake its twisting way alone. The heavy white head faced them, its black empty eye sockets seeming filled with power. Seastrider snorted with a wild awe, planted her feet on the thin ledge, and folded her wings in a gesture of deference. Teb slid down and approached the skeleton. Neither his gaze nor Seastrider's left the dark shadows of those hollow eyes.

This was why they had come.

Teb slipped the lyre from inside his tunic.

As if in answer to his gesture, he heard Meriden cry, *Yes, give the lyre to Bayzun.*

This was why she had led him here.

Bayzun's great feet stood solidly, one with the claws torn away. From these had the lyre been carved. Teb knelt. He knew with a calm certainty that if the lyre was returned to the bones of Bayzun, the lyre's power would become immense.

Yes, give him the lyre, Tebriel.

But as he reached to place the lyre before Bayzun, Seastrider swung her head and pushed him aside. "Wait."

He glared at her, startled.

Meriden's voice was insistent. *Give Bayzun the lyre, Teb. There is little time—our soldiers are losing. Listen to your bard knowledge. Bayzun is the grandfather of all dragons. If you lay the lyre at Bayzun's feet, the power will come.*

"*Is* that bard knowledge, Tebriel?" Seastrider said. "*Is* that Meriden's voice?"

He stared at her. "Of course!"

But now Meriden shouted, *Do not part with it! Do not give it!*

Teb stood up, confused, and stared around him, clutching the lyre.

Make the Ivory Lyre speak, Tebriel. But do not give it. Bring Bayzun's power alive with its song.

Which was Meriden?

Which was the dark?

One voice was false—but how clearly it imitated hers.

Yet surely he had only to make one simple gesture, had only to lay the lyre at Bayzun's feet, and he could resurrect the lyre's power. There was no evil in Bayzun, only the power of the light.

Do not let the lyre from your hand! the voice cried.

He looked at Seastrider, sick with uncertainty.

Lay the lyre at the feet of Bayzun, Tebriel. Do not play it now, in this place. Give the lyre to Bayzun. . . .

Surely that was Meriden.

Make the lyre speak, Teb, do not give it. Sing Bayzun alive, sing his power alive.

The voices dueling inside his head dizzied him. He plucked one string so hard the little lyre shook. . . .

But it was silent.

He stared at it, shocked into choking dismay. He had used its strength too recently, to save himself in the drug dens of Sharden.

They needed the lyre now, more than Tirror had ever needed it. Shame held him. Terror held him.

You must renew its strength, Tebriel—at the feet of Bayzun.

Yes. Yes. That was Meriden's voice.

27

Cries of battle echoed through the cave. Teb saw visions of animals falling and arrows piercing the diving dragons. He saw Snowblitz thrashing with a bleeding wing and saw the dark unliving striding among the fallen, tasting gore, swinging their swords and laughing. He tried to bring power with his own voice, with song. Sweating, choking, he could hardly use his cracking voice. The lyre remained silent.

There is only one way, Tebriel. Give the lyre to Bayzun. There it can regain its strength. Our armies are dying, Teb.

He had failed Tirror twice, failed them all. He must not fail now. He stood staring at Bayzun's skeleton and could do nothing. Bayzun stared back at him, seeming engorged with eerie power.

Did not Bayzun command him to return the lyre? Why else was he here, but to return it? Again he knelt before the skeleton. What harm could come from Bayzun? He held out the lyre, reaching. . . .

But something stopped him, made him draw back. This was not the way. . . .

Thakkur's words thundered in his memory. *Do not underestimate Quazelzeg.* . . .

He must trust nothing. To give the lyre from his grasp, in these endless and alien worlds, could risk everything. In one final, false step, he could give Quazelzeg and the dark a terrible power. Visions of the battle surged. He turned.

He saw Meriden astride her dragon, winging down the well of sky toward him.

But suddenly the dragon was gone. Meriden was falling, alone, falling through the endless cleft . . . falling . . . falling alone reaching out to him. *Do not give the lyre.* Dark winds tumbled her and flung her down chasms; boulders spun and bounced against her.

Quazelzeg's voice exploded. *"Give the lyre to Bayzun, and I will release her."*

"No!" she cried. *"You will destroy everything!"*

"Let her go!" Teb shouted. *"I will NOT give the lyre! Release her!"* But his voice choked with uncertainty.

Meriden was pulled through shifting winds and swept crashing into stone. She was pressed between stone walls so tight she was nearly crushed, could not lift her arms, stone crushing her cheek, twisting her body. . . .

"Give me the lyre!"

"I will NOT! Release her!" But he was shaking with terror for her.

Suddenly the rock exploded, throwing her into space

again. Quazelzeg's laugh was terrible, thundering echoing as she fell careening among pieces of the mountain. Visions of battle clashed around Meriden's falling figure. The armies of light were pulling back. The whole of the universe seemed filled with the dark's swelling power.

He must make the lyre speak. He *must*.

He tried, straining, and could not.

"Give the lyre! Save your mother! Save Tirror!"

Defeat filled him. He had no choice. He could not let her die—even for Tirror. He stared at Bayzun's mutilated toes, from which the lyre had been carved.

"No, Teb! No!"

How could he help but give it? He reached out with the lyre . . . .

Quazelzeg appeared suddenly, blocking the skeleton, pulling the lyre from him. . . .

"No!" He struck Quazelzeg's hands from the lyre, broke his grip with one sharp blow, knocked the unman down as he jerked the lyre away. He *shouted* a bard's song at Quazelzeg, wrought of all the pain and love in him. A terrible power of love rose out of him, a power he had nearly denied, love for Tirror, love for all the world he had nearly lost—love for his mother and what she was and for all those close to him. They would be nothing if Tirror were lost, they would all be lost, Meriden destroyed. In that moment of terrible understanding, his hands struck the strings again and the lyre sang out fierce and wild with love.

But in the moment that Quazelzeg had held the lyre, a rift had been torn between worlds. Quazelzeg's laughter thundered. "Too late! Useless! Too late—the Doors are open now!" Teb saw the hordes pouring through onto the battlefield. A blood-faced shade scuttled through. A vulture with a woman's eyes fled through. Too late. . . . The barrier had been torn. The dark hordes came rushing. Doors flung open across a thousand worlds and a black mass of monsters poured into Tirror, leaping onto the backs of the retreating armies, slashing at the horses' legs. The lyre's song rang out, and the attack faltered—but not enough. From every palace window and door, dark incubi and blood-licking demons crawled and flew, howling, reaching. The air was a tangle of screams and groans and stinks. Quazelzeg's laughter thundered. "Too late, too late . . ." A young otter was stabbed, screaming. Monstrous vultures snatched up foxes and wolves.

"No!" Teb shouted. "No!" Not even the lyre was stopping them. "Bayzun!" he shouted. The lyre wailed. He prayed to the Graven Light, and he prayed to Bayzun. He slapped the silver strings with a love for Tirror that nearly tore him apart. The lyre's voice rang so mightily he could feel it stinging his blood; suddenly it shouted a dragon's raging bellow, and Teb shouted with it, "*Bayzun!*"

Bayzun's skeleton vanished. The huge black dragon loomed over him, its breath blazing, its eyes like fire.

The voice of the lyre was Bayzun's voice. The black dragon exploded past him out of the cave on immense wings, his red mouth open in a bull dragon's bellow. Teb turned, playing the lyre with all the power in him, and Meriden was there astride Dawncloud, rocking on Bayzun's wind beside the cave door.

"Now!" she cried. "Now . . ."

Teb leaped for Seastrider and felt Seastrider's excitement, felt the closeness of the two dragons, mother and child. The lyre's voice thundered as the dragons wheeled together up the cleft, following Bayzun. Where—where was a way through . . . ?

It was that moment, in vision, that Teb saw Thakkur fighting something dark and grinning, saw the white otter's sword flash, saw him back the vampire-toothed demon away with snarling rage and drive his sword in; but too late—Teb cried out as Thakkur was struck from behind, as Thakkur fell. . . .

Thakkur . . .

And Teb could not reach him.

"There," Meriden cried, pointing where a bright thin crack appeared in murky space. "There . . ." Bayzun was through. They plunged after him—and dropped into the sky above the battle.

Teb searched wildly for Thakkur. Bayzun dove, slashing at the unliving. Meriden's sword flashed. Teb brought the lyre's song ringing across the battle to drive the dark back. The lyre's roar and Bayzun's roar filled the wind. He saw the dark falter—and he searched for one small white figure amid the surging battle.

The dark fell back. Rebel warriors rose to storm palace walls. Monsters seething over parapets dropped down again into the courtyard, their screeching silenced.

Nightraider dove at a tangle of giant serpents; Camery slashed and cut at them. Ebis the Black rode down a screaming basilisk and cut its snake body to shreds. The great cats and wolves tore at the unliving. Dragons dove to burn. Marshy leaned down, clutching harness, to snatch up a wounded otter. The lyre's song thundered across the battlefield, driving back the dark— but it was Bayzun who struck the coldest terror into the dark forces.

On a hilltop, Windcaller fought to drive warriors away from Kiri, who knelt, cradling Thakkur.

She had seen the hordes of dark monsters appear from nowhere, storming out of the palace. In that moment when defeat was certain, she had seen Thakkur fall. Windcaller had cut a swath through the attacking hordes, and Kiri had knelt over Thakkur in the little space Windcaller won. She held Thakkur's body, trying to find a heartbeat. There was none. She rocked him, torn with grief for him, sick with despair.

Their world was dying, Tirror was dying. There would be nothing left but the dark. Teb was lost somewhere. Kiri's stomach was twisted in knots. Thakkur's poor torn body seemed an instrument of terrible prediction, mirroring the final and terrible end for them all.

Then something stirred her. Something summoned.

She heard the lyre crying out across the battle, silencing all cries with its fury. She saw the black dragon explode out of nothing, riderless and huge. She saw Seastrider . . . and Teb! She saw a white dragon she had never seen. A woman—Meriden!

The lyre thundered. The black dragon slaughtered. The rebel armies rallied, and the dark armies trembled and fell back as Kiri knelt on the battlefield, holding Thakkur and screaming with victory.

Teb saw her crouched before Windcaller, holding something white. He sped toward them, leaped down, and knelt beside Kiri praying that Thakkur was alive.

And knowing he was not.

Kiri and Teb cradled Thakkur between them, their eyes meeting in a storm of grief.

She smoothed Thakkur's bloody white fur over his terrible wound. Teb pulled Kiri against his shoulder suddenly and fiercely, and held her tight, Thakkur couched in their circling arms.

When Teb rose at last, he held Thakkur gently. He turned away from Kiri to mount Seastrider. Kiri watched as they lifted away above the battle. She did not follow.

In the sky, Teb cradled Thakkur's body inside his tunic, beneath the lyre. He stroked the lyre's strings in a thundering dirge for Thakkur, its voice struck with grief and love. At its bright, ringing notes, the last of the dark hordes turned and fled into the palace. They pushed back through Quazelzeg's golden Door, trampling each other, wraiths and incubi and monsters crowding through.

Among the dark warriors, only Quazelzeg paused.

When all the hordes had fled, Quazelzeg stood within the safety of the gold Door, burning with fury at what he had lost.

But there would be other worlds, other challenges. He turned to consider such worlds—his next quest.

He went white at what he saw.

He spun and tried to run, but light exploded around him, light so bright and consuming that the Door was lost in its brilliance. The light twisted Quazelzeg and sucked him in. He spun within its glow, screaming. . . .

Slowly he was consumed, by a light so powerful that it turned white the battlefield and the surrounding hills, and its clear brilliance burst like a nova across Tirror's skies.

The terror of Quazelzeg's scream remained long after his body was consumed. The light that took him was seen from Auric Palace in an exploding brilliance that cascaded across the sky; it was seen in Nightpool, where the few otters who had remained stared up in chittering wonder.

It turned the sky over Yoorthed so pale that the dwarfs ran out of the cave, shouting, "What is it?"

"Power," King Flam said, staring at the shining sky.

"What power?" a dwarf said, shivering.

"Not the power of the dark," King Flam cried, his voice thundering. He smiled at the gathered dwarfs.

"I would guess the battle has ended. This," King Flam said, sighing with relief, "this is the greatest power—the power that holds us all."

28

The battlefield was still, every face turned toward the Graven Light. Not until that light faded did anyone speak, and then only in whispers.

"*We* did not kill Quazelzeg. . . ."

"The light . . ."

"The Graven Light . . ."

They moved at last, to kneel beside their wounded. They tended some wounded on the battlefield and carried the most grievously hurt to the palace. The voice of the lyre had stilled. The spirit of Bayzun was gone, back into the centuries. When the mortal dragons glided down to the palace, Seastrider, Windcaller, Nightraider and Starpounder crowded around their mother, bellowing and slapping their wings over her. They had been only dragonlings when Dawncloud had left them to search for Meriden. The bards slid down, laughing, amid the tangle of wings and sparring dragons. Teb turned away and went directly into the palace, carrying the body of Thakkur safe beneath his tunic.

Camery hugged her mother so hard Meriden gasped, laughing and hugging her back. They looked at each other silently, each seeing something of herself. Meriden touched Camery's face, her hair.

"It's still pale gold. I used to braid it all down your back. And when you rode, little wisps would come loose."

"And when you washed it, I cried."

Meriden laughed. "You had a tantrum, sometimes, when I washed your hair. Oh, you did cry. And—and when I went away," Meriden said, "I cried. I had lost you—and Teb—and my true love." She wept again, and they held each other for a long time.

Teb found tools in the palace and went alone across the hills to cut a straight oak. He hewed out a coffin for Thakkur and laid him in it, his whole being filled with grieving. He nailed on the lid and carried the coffin to the hill where he had first come with Seastrider. There he piled boulders around it until he could give Thakkur a proper burial. When he came down the hill, Meriden was waiting for him. He saw in her eyes clear knowledge of his pain.

Teb held her, needing her as if he were a child again. As they clung together, it might have been, again, that windy fall morning when he was small and she had held him and said good-bye.

He said, "I read your journal."

"Yes."

"How did you make the entries that . . . came later?"

Her eyes widened. "I . . . wasn't sure I could. I hoped that maybe . . ." She shook her head, smiling.

"There are such powers beyond this world, Teb. I hoped . . . I wrote messages with spring water—on the ground, on stone walls, anywhere, because I was so lonely sometimes. As if writing words could link me to you. One message—the last message—I prayed that you would see that."

She gave him a cool, steady look. "The diary pages I wrote when you were small—I was wrong not to tell you and Camery that you were dragonbards. I was as wrong as the unliving, who kept the true history from Tirror."

"No. It was different. You meant to save us pain."

"Not at all different. I took your own history from you. I did it to save you, but the result is the same."

"You must not feel that. If anyone has been foolish, I have."

She put her fingers over his lips and kissed his forehead. "Quazelzeg is dead. The force that we battled is gone. That's all that matters. The power of the unliving is gone . . . from this world." She took his face in her hands, and her green eyes were very alive.

"There are other bards, Teb. Beyond the Doors. So far away . . . lost out there. They could come home, find their way home now that the unliving are gone. There are other creatures also," she said, "wanting to come through—to come home. Unicorns, Teb. And . . . there are dragons."

"Dragons," he said, his thoughts filled with Kiri's longing.

"Dragons that search for their bards." She studied his face, touched his thoughts, and smiled. "A dragon the color of seas, who yearns for a bard he says is of Tirror."

Teb's heart quickened.

"A dark-haired girl," Meriden said. "He says she is called by the name of a bird."

"A wren!" Teb shouted.

"Yes," Meriden said, smiling.

He laughed out loud with pleasure. "The great cats call her Kiri wren—a love name."

"The dragons will come," she said. "The dragons will find their way—that dragon certainly will—and the bards will. But now . . ."

She turned, and when Teb looked, there were unicorns on the hill around them, moving delicately, their horns as bright as sun on water. They pushed around Meriden, nuzzling her. Their scent was like honey, their fine muscled bodies warm and silken to stroke. They nosed at Teb and rubbed their bright horns against his shoulder. But soon they began to move out onto the battlefield, to nose and touch the wounded, to heal where they could heal.

Teb and Meriden made their way to the palace. They knelt with Kiri and Camery over wounded soldiers and animals, to doctor their hurts. Mitta was there, washing away blood, applying poultices and sewing torn flesh. Hanni knew about Thakkur. He clung close to Mitta, helping her, his small face desolate with grief.

The wounded kept coming, hobbling or carried. The bards housed them in the palace courtyard and in the main hall, tearing down ornate draperies to make soft beds. Ebis and his soldiers made stretchers from palace furniture and brought in the most seriously injured, though Ebis himself limped from his wounds. Camery rebound his leg where the bandages were soaked with blood. She thought he should soak it with poultices, but he said he hadn't time. He went back to the wounded again, and not long afterward he returned to the hall carrying Charkky, the little otter pressed against his black beard shivering with pain.

"His shoulder is badly torn," Ebis said, kneeling to lay Charkky on a blanket. The bards knelt around Charkky. Teb examined him as gently as he could. Charkky gritted his teeth when Camery cleaned the wound. Teb held Charkky's paws while Camery pulled the torn flesh together and stitched it up. Even when the needle went in, Charkky tried his best not to yell. Instead he bit Teb hard on the thumb.

Afterward, he stared at Teb, chagrined.

"It's all right," Teb said. "You couldn't help it."

"I never dreamed in all my life I would bite you, Tebriel. Tease you, maybe, hold you under the water, but not bite you." He looked around. "Where is Mikk?"

"Here," Mikk said. "I came to find you. Hah! You look like a fine warrior in that bandage." Mikk knelt and stared with concern into Charkky's face. Hanni came to press against them. Mikk gathered up the little white otter and held him tight.

The palace hall grew crowded with the wounded, both human and animal. Kiri rose from doctoring a rebel soldier and stood watching Teb. She knew he grieved for Thakkur, and took his hand. They stood looking over the crowded hall. There was nothing she could say to ease his terrible remorse. He would never heal from it. She couldn't change what had happened; she could only be there for him, be close to him.

When Teb turned away to help Colewolf with a wounded child, Kiri saw two cats carried in, limp and bleeding, and was riven with fear, again, for Elmmira. She went to search, though she had looked and looked across the battlefield for the tawny cat.

She and Windcaller scanned the body-strewn fields and hills. They saw Mmenimm, saw Aven and Marshy carrying in a fox and two owls. Windcaller circled, working farther away from the palace, until they saw a pale buff cat among the boats of the harbor. Kiri leaned down with relief to call to Elmmira.

The big cat was dragging an un-man from a sailing boat. Two captains lay on the shore. When Windcaller dropped down, Kiri saw the bloody claw marks slashed deep through their yellow tunics. She thought the one with the greasy hair was Captain Vighert. She slid down and went to look, but suddenly she felt weak and dizzy, as if everything was catching up with her. Elmmira came to her. Kiri knelt, to lean against Elmmira's warm shoulder.

"It's all right now, Kiri wren. It's all over now."

"I know, Elmmira." She looked into Elmmira's golden eyes. Elmmira always made her feel better. The great cat licked her face. "You are tired, Kiri wren."

"I never thought Teb would return. When we first got to Aquervell and came down on that hill, and he was gone, I thought . . ."

"But he did return." Elmmira purred loudly. "It's all right now, Kiri wren." She drew back, her whiskers twitching. "Tebriel is looking for you."

Kiri turned, to see Seastrider banking along the shore. The white dragon dropped toward them and settled beside Windcaller. Teb reached down to take Kiri's hand.

"Come, sit on Seastrider's back."

She looked up at him, puzzled.

"Come on."

Windcaller nuzzled her shoulder, then lifted away toward the sea. *Hungry*, she called back. *I'm going fishing. . . .*

Kiri climbed up in front of Teb. It was strange to be on another dragon. Teb was warm against her, his arms strong and warm around her. They sat close for a long time, not saying much. After a while, he said, "I have a surprise for you."

237

"What?"

"I won't tell you. We'll show you."

Seastrider snorted and rose fast into the wind. Kiri could feel the white dragon's delight, but what kind of surprise would so please a dragon? They banked toward the mountain ridge that rose north of the palace. It shone dark now, against the dropping sun, streaked with deep black ridges along the mountain's face. Seastrider winged close, into the heavy shadows. Kiri stared, puzzled—but her heart had begun to pound crazily.

"There," she cried suddenly. "Oh!"

A dragon exploded out of the shadows—a big, strapping dragon. He banked so close to them that his wind rocked Seastrider, and his wings brushed Kiri's face. He was sea colored, blue and green and shimmering. He swept by, staring at Kiri with eyes of green fire. He winged close again, stretched out his long neck and handsome head, and breathed his warm breath across her face. He smelled of spices and of the salty sea. She stared into his eyes, laughing, crying, wild with things she could not express. "Varuna," she whispered. "Your name is Varuna!"

He matched his wings with Seastrider's so his body rocked against the white dragon, and Kiri climbed onto his back and snuggled down between his wings.

When she looked over at Teb, her face was filled with a wonder and glory that turned him warm with love for her.

"How . . . ?" she began.

"He came through the Doors," Teb said. "After you left to search for Elmmira. He was suddenly there in the sky beside Seastrider, when she and the dragonlings went to feed."

Kiri lay down along Varuna's neck. As he lifted away, she blew Teb a wild, ecstatic kiss. The green dragon swept up, and up, and broke through the cloud cover. They disappeared up there, into a world silent and private.

29

OUR MOST VIVID MOMENTS MAKE ACTUAL FOR US THE
MYSTERY OF OUR EXISTENCE IN THIS WORLD. BUT IT
IS DRAGON SONG THAT BRINGS ALIVE THE MYSTERY
OF THE PAST WITHIN US.
From the diary of meriden, Queen of Auric,
written after her return to Auric

———⟨∞⟩———

For nine days the army of light remained in Sharden's city, trying to mend itself. The unicorns moved
among the wounded, healing those they could heal.
But nearly every day there was someone to bury. The
townsfolk brought bread and fruits, meat and milk,
but there were not enough herbs for medicine, not
enough healing skill even with the unicorns' magic.

Teb spent most of his time with Charkky and Hanni,
for, while Charkky was nearly well, Hanni was not.
The little otter lay huddled next to Charkky, his small
white face filled with grieving. Many otters fished for

him, but he wouldn't eat. Meriden was with him often, and the unicorns came to kneel around him. They licked his white face and made what magic they could, but Hanni's grief seemed beyond healing. His silent cry echoed in Teb's mind, and when the small otter overheard plans for Thakkur's burial ceremony, he was nearly hysterical.

"No! Thakkur is not dead! Thakkur cannot die!"

"Hush," the unicorns said. "Hush." They stood touching Hanni with their horns, the gentle bright beasts giving what magic they could. But they could not heal him.

Meriden knelt before Hanni and took the golden sphere from her throat. She hung the chain around the small otter's neck, where it lay gleaming against his white fur. "Do you know what this sphere means, Hanni?"

"En-endless life," Hanni said. "The endless sphere of life."

"Exactly." Meriden sighed and pushed back her tawny hair. "You are Thakkur's heir, Hanni. Only you can carry on that endless thread for Thakkur. Do you understand how much Thakkur counted on you to do that?"

Tears coursed down Hanni's face.

"If you do not do this for Thakkur, you will surely condemn him to a true death. Only you can make Thakkur's power live, now, on Tirror."

Hanni stared at her.

She looked up at Teb. "Sing, Tebriel. Sing of the island of Nightpool."

Teb wove a song of Nightpool so luminous that the unicorns stared up at him with longing. He brought alive the clear green sea foaming white against the black cliffs, showering salty spray into the caves. He showed the young otter cubs bobbing and shouting in the surf, otters napping in the kelp beds and diving to the deep sea valleys awash in clear green light. He showed the undersea world with its mountains and shadows and forests of waving sea plants so powerfully that all who listened could feel the sweep of the tides and hear the sea pounding in their ears. He made a song of Thakkur's cave, its shelves filled with the white otter's sea treasures, all his shells and coins, and the big ugly skull of the shark.

He made the song of the world's beginning, wove it from bard knowledge, but also with the wisdom that Thakkur had imparted in its telling: the spinning ball of gases formed by such infinite and wondrous power that no creature could know its true nature, the five huge continents, the flood, the many small island continents that remained. He sang Thakkur's words of hope, of faith.

Hanni listened, weeping, pressing against Charkky and Mikk. But when Mikk lifted Hanni's chin, the small otter looked stronger. A spark of resolve had begun to burn. From that moment, Hanni began to mend.

On the day of burial, the bards and otters made Hanni an important part of the ceremony.

All the human troops and animals met in the square in the center of the city. Here they buried their dead, the speaking animals and humans side by side. There would be a marker for them, wrought by Sharden's old stonecutters. Only Thakkur had a separate grave, and he would have a special marker. Another like it would stand in Nightpool. His life would be known and remembered in bardsong and carved into stone as well.

When the armies gathered around his grave, it was Hanni alone who said the prayer for him, a quiet prayer that left everyone silent for a long time afterward, kneeling around the grave. The bards planted wild herbs on Thakkur's grave, those he had loved best. They left the grave touched by sun that warmed the small flowers and teased a spicy scent from them.

As the armies made their way back through the city toward the palace and hills, people everywhere were cleaning, scrubbing walls and floors and pavements, burning refuse, tearing down, starting to build anew. The unicorns moved among them, healing the sick and drug-ridden: Already a thread of the old magic had begun to spin itself through Tirror.

The next day, when the rebels left Sharden, the unicorns disappeared into the hills of Aquervell. Some were seen later swimming the strait to Ekthuma. Much later they appeared in the sanctuaries of Gardel-Cloor and Nison-Serth, the sanctuary at Nightpool, all the sacred places. Their long exile had made them elusive creatures—but they were home again.

The journey home for most of the army was slow. The owls flew ahead to spread the news to those who had stayed behind, to the sick and old and those who must care for the livestock. For the bards and the Nightpool otters, the journey was so fast that the sights and feel of Sharden's city were still with them when they settled onto the sea around Nightpool. The otters piled off the dragons' backs, thankful to be home, though it was not a pleasant homecoming.

What had been planned as the otters' homecoming ceremony for Thakkur was a time of terrible grieving. The bards knelt with the otters before Thakkur's dais in the sacred cave. Hanni, using all the strength he possessed, stood whispering his few practiced words in a final farewell. But suddenly there was a hush of breath from the gathered otters, and they stared at something behind him. He turned and raised a paw in shock. Then he reached toward the shell and stood with his paw outstretched, as still as a small white statue.

The sacred shell had begun to glow. A white mist shone; then Thakkur looked out at them. His silent voice was clear and strong.

This is not good-bye; death is not good-bye. We will know one another again, for life is a journey without ending. Like the sphere that Hanni now wears, all life is endless.

Tirror is at peace, Thakkur said. *Know joy, take joy in this world, as I will in the worlds I now enter.*

"Go in peace," Hanni whispered as the vision faded. "Go with joy and love. Walk with me again, Thakkur . . . somewhere."

As they filed out of the sacred cave, Kiri's hand in Teb's, she said softly, "He'll be all right now."

Teb nodded and leaned to brush away her tears.

Not long afterward, the eight bards, with hugs for the otters, and many promises about the days to come, leaped from the cliff to the backs of the dragons and rose in a thunder of wings. The dragons circled Nightpool, then swept for Auric Palace, along the rocky coast, dropping low beside the small coastal towns. The townsfolk who had remained behind ran out of their cottages shouting excited greetings.

"The dragons!"

"The dragons are back! The bards have returned!"

"Tebriel . . ."

"Camery . . ."

Then a silence of surprise touched the villagers, for Dawncloud had banked low, and they could see Meriden.

"The queen . . ."

"The queen lives!"

"*Meriden!*"

"Praise the queen!"

"Praise the Graven Light. . . ."

Wild cheering rose from friends she had not seen for many years, and she raised her arm in salute. At once riders started out at a gallop for the palace to greet her.

The dragons came down beside the palace wall and left their bards amid shouting and laughing friends. The moment Meriden dismounted, she was swept up and lifted high above the crowd. Four soldiers carried her into the palace.

When she saw the hall, her face was filled with such mixed emotions that all the crowd went still.

Pain was in her face, longing. A tangle of memories of the king. She went to the hearth and knelt beside the crock of fresh bay leaves and smelled them. Someone had remembered that she had always kept the spicy-scented leaves there. She moved around the room, looking.

When she turned back to the hearth, she laid her hand on the rough stone, and her thought touched the bards sharply. This palace had stood for many generations before the coming of the dark. It would stand long after the dark was only a memory. She unbuckled her scabbard and sword and hung them on the hook that, so long ago, the King of Auric had used. Then she gathered Teb and Camery to her. Teb reached for Kiri. Colewolf pulled the three children close. The bards stood together within the calm safety of Auric Palace.

It would be many months before Meriden would tell them about all of her life for those exiled years. It would be many years before Tirror would recover completely from its long siege. But that recovery had begun.

"We will bring all who want to come here to the palace," Meriden said. "The sick to heal, and the orphans, just as Garit has done at Dacia. We will help teach them crafts, soldiering, whatever they wish." She looked evenly at the bards. "We must keep a strong army. The dark has proven this—that the powers of bards and dragons alone are not enough."

Teb hugged her, liking very much this person who was his mother.

"Perhaps we could join with Ebis the Black," Camery said, "in training our young warriors and in defending Windthorst."

"Perhaps we could," Meriden said. "I think you make a good captain, my daughter. I think you would work well with Ebis."

The hall had grown crowded. Meriden looked around at her friends. "The old sanctuaries—Nison-Serth, Gardel-Cloor—all will be way stations again, gathering places for all speaking animals and all humans." Her face brightened, her eyes smiling. "We are free again—to travel as we wish. Each of us is free, to live how and where we wish." She turned from them and went to stand before the hearth. When she turned back, every eye was on her.

"There are other worlds," Meriden said, "that the slave masters have fought again and again to conquer. Those worlds that have held fast their freedom cherish that freedom well."

She shook her head. "Tirror had never known that

kind of challenge—until Quazelzeg and his disciples invaded us.

"Now . . . I think that now everyone on Tirror must find some way to join with the bards. I think that we must all work together, to remain free of those like the unliving."

Teb stood, at dusk, in Auric's tower. He raised a hand to Kiri in the courtyard, and she ran up the stairs to him. They stood close, leaning on the stone wall, looking out over the green meadows and the sea, watching the dragons. Some of them were winging over the sea lithe as swallows, diving for sharks. But Varuna and the dragonlings were stretched out across the meadow, their wings tucked close to their bodies, surrounded by calmly grazing horses.

"Varuna is telling the dragonlings of other worlds," Kiri said. She turned to look at Teb. "He's the most wonderful dragon in any world."

Teb grinned at her. "He's wild—fiery. He's a fine dragon. The dragonlings are very impressed; all the dragons are. I know Seastrider's thoughts about him. Really very admiring."

She laughed. "I'd call Windcaller's thoughts amorous."

He smiled. "They can have some life of their own now—we all can."

"You told me once you used to dream of dragons here, on the meadows of Auric."

"I did. A sight just like that, with fine horses grazing among them, unafraid. I used to dream a lot of things about this land, and what I hoped it would be like someday." He put his arm around her. "I used to dream about sharing it with someone. But I didn't know who."

"Do you know now?"

"Yes. I know now."

She brushed her lips across his cheek, warm in his arms, and their minds saw and felt as one.